COSMOPORT

MARK DEKLERK BUHLER

Writers Apex

Gateway Towards Success

8063 MADISON AVE #1252
Indianapolis, IN 46227
+13176596889
www.writersapex.com

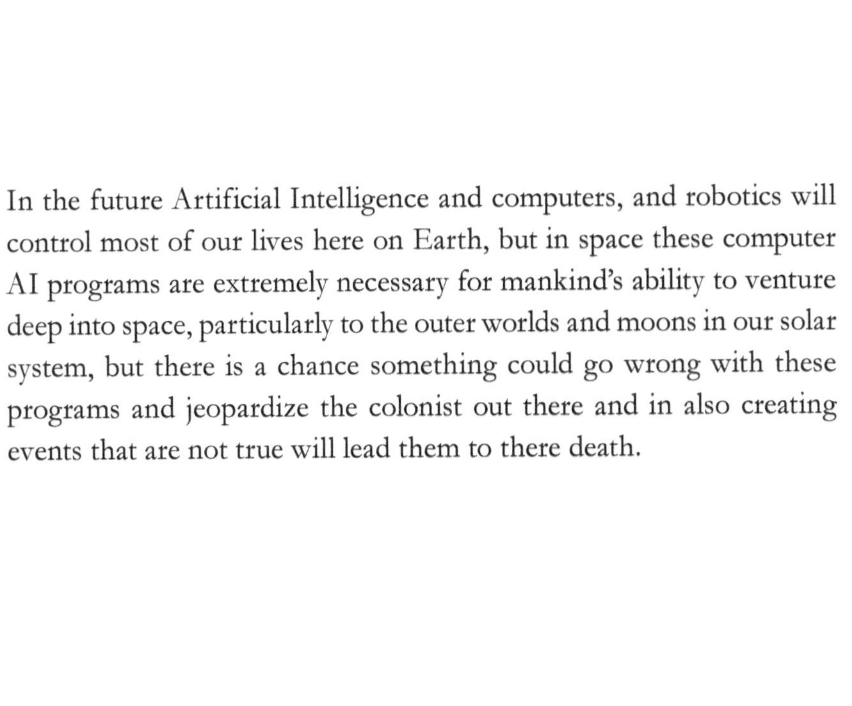

In the future Artificial Intelligence and computers, and robotics will control most of our lives here on Earth, but in space these computer AI programs are extremely necessary for mankind's ability to venture deep into space, particularly to the outer worlds and moons in our solar system, but there is a chance something could go wrong with these programs and jeopardize the colonist out there and in also creating events that are not true will lead them to there death.

Mark DeKlerk Buhler

BIOGRAPHY

Mark DeKlerk Buhler is an avid fan of science fiction and author in writing this story to me was fantastic in portraying scientific possibilities of a human stationing base on Triton, and I hope the reader will enjoy this from beginning to the end and support mankind's vision to explore the outer planets and moons of this incredible solar system now and in the years to come.

A 2215 TRITON NEPTUNE STORY

By Mark De Klerk Buhler

The Extreme cold moon of Triton at our early settlement base we named Cosmoport to the stars on a cantaloupe hilly terrain in the far sided edge of our sun's solar system looking out into deep space with Neptune Pluto and Charon in their wonder from our new Triton base multi-function telescope, and dish telescope by providing our distant, but nearby look at 'Alpha-Centauri our next door neighbor in the next solar system', in our space date time of April, 2215.

On September 2213, the cargo freighter 'New Day', came to an orbit around the moon Triton and will stay in orbit until the 'venture', spacecraft will appear in the near future and rendezvous with it in November 2213 Earth time and from there the space crew will establish a new more sturdy colony settlement called, 'Cosmoport base', on a chosen predetermined moon site with the construction that will mostly quickly be made by robots from the 'Venture', spacecraft that will be in the Triton orbit and when almost finished they will land and setup the remainder site on the surface and once done their work will only just have begun when they will finish a new modular expansion settlement outpost for future scientists and people who are willing to pay a lot to live in a new form of rustic outerworld private accommodations in seeing Pluto, Charon and Neptune, and with Neptune, which is ninety percent and constantly appearing quite large and magnificent overhead at the 'Cosmoport base'.

Our scientific, mining research, and astronomical settlement was designed to look out into the Kuiper belt and also with this moon we are looking for objects and possibilities of any life here at this recently created settlement base and with our hard work, and its possible finding rich resources that we can take back to Earth in the near future.

<u>What we know and have learned from our stay here on Triton</u>

- Earth to Neptune is in astronomical units is 29.09 or 2,703,959,960 miles taking roughly almost three years at 150,000 constant MPH
- Has a slightly stronger magnetic field than moons in the solar system
- Nitrogen, methane and sample amounts of carbon monoxide and trace amounts of extreme frozen water
- One Triton day > equals 6 Earth days or TRINEP 6-1, spacetime
- Cosmoport base facing Neptune always
- Light or radio signals take up to four hours to reach Triton
- Has a Cantaloupe mountainous or hilly terrain and straight plains similar to nitrogen water ice oceans and a subsurface volcano activity
- Gravity is 0.08 compared to the Earth's moon of 0.15, Earth 1.0
- Outside top surface temperature is minus 391 degrees fahrenheit
- Subsurface temperature is not colder than 38 degrees fahrenh.
- Jumping six to seven feet and running fast is easy here on Triton
- Its atmosphere and pressure is only 14 microbars and is mostly composed mainly of nitrogen and other trace elements with its atmosphere reaching to 800 kilometers or 497 miles above, to its exobase from the moon surface.
- It takes over three years for a rocket ship to travel from Earth to Triton.

Five years ago we came here to Triton, instead of going to Pluto because we believe by being here we can view Neptune, Triton and the Kuiper belt in equal detail and being closure to the sun's orbit in providing

Earth with all its important information about this outer moon, and also with it's possible mining of these outer planets and moons far from our sun and why we can and should explore Triton as to what kind of moon it is constituted on the top surface and its below subsurface alike.

Our transportation here was with the our Interplanetary AX5 Quad Thorium Nuclear Powered Vessel, called the 'Venture', spaceship that took us almost three years at speeds of a variable eighty-five to one hundred thousand miles per hour of the almost three billion miles in reaching this moon Triton and looking back towards our sun it looks like just another slightly bigger stars in the cosmos with this moon being extremely cold with occasional falling and drifting nitrogen and methane snow with carbon monoxide and traces of extreme frozen water. It looks like Antarctica but worse in the wintertime, but in being here with these very extreme cold temperatures and a cold frost surface with a mainly nitrogen lined atmosphere of 14 microbars.

We have a special extreme payload heavy duty cold weather nuclear powered track vehicle that we are able to use here and it can only take us about twenty to thirty miles before we have to return it back here to warm the vehicle up, otherwise the vehicle will crack and be completely damaged with no tow truck here on Triton we could be in serious trouble here at this settlement base for staying out here in this frigid cold with our space suits that will survive us only good enough for not more than fifteen to twenty maybe twenty five minutes at a time, with our oxygen mixture and battery supply providing our breathing and warmth and power that will run out quickly in exposing us to a very cold death of almost minus four hundred fahrenheit degrees here on this moon Triton.

Our spaceship 'Venture', is orbiting Triton at about one hundred and twenty-five thousand feet straight up from our settlement base called 'Cosmoport', in providing our base now with direct link communications with Earth Space Command and in giving us a radar and optical view of one thousand mile radius of our settlement base here with perfect clarity, and the spacecraft can also provide us with GPS signal coordinates to our nuclear powered mobile track vehicle or our capsule shuttle space pods with its two thousand mile range, if we have to go anywhere from our base here at our cantaloupe terrain contoured base, with Cosmoport, we can do that easily and safely. It is important to note that gravity here on this moon is quite light on our bodies, a strong exercise program is encouraged in our graviton exercise pod unit to have a workout of at least every Earth day of 24 hours for at least one hour in our rotating centrifugal graviton wheel workout pod.

TRINEP 6-1 spacetime, equals 6 Earth Days to one Triton Day.

When we came here there was waiting for us a special robotic spaceship, we call the 'Factory', with all kinds of stuff for our needs in housing, laboratory and greenhouse modules, building materials and our own kind of robotic infrastructure module assembly system setup here in Triton orbit so we can direct its manufacture on Triton's surface, so as to create our base easily here on Triton we named Cosmoport,, with each module part we call SHOPs that had to land extremely near each other on the surface to place together carefully from up here with our specialized four robotic industrial construction 8 legged walking sticks and our one heavy duty nuclear track vehicle that we directed from Triton orbit, and we had no choice but to spend almost three Earth months in space orbit to remotely do this through our AI robotic remote control assembly by our track vehicle and modules to build and assemble together like a jigsaw puzzle part a fitting into part b and so forth. Because of the light gravity here, assembling these structures was quite easy for us.

And, when it was roboticaly completed in our real time operations here in space with our last orbiting of this moon we then landed and set up and completed our habitat and equipment on this surface for our possible ten years stay here before we can return back to Earth with our human and android crew replacements coming from Earth with our data and results of Triton for them to see and add on in their new stay here for them to continue our work that we began.

TRINEP, 0-0 spacetime

My name is Franz Waldheim, chief supervisory geologist and chemist of this cantaloupe terrain Cosmoport, SHOP, Moon Complex, I am chief director of Cosmoport base here, and my team and I are well along with our mining by our very talented scientist astronaut crew that have now penetrated almost one hundred feet of this moon's permafrost crust of mostly basalt frozen methane and nitrogen with trace amounts of oxygen and even smaller amounts of carbon monoxide and carbon dioxide and with this moon also containing large amounts of permafrost and granite condensed crystallized water ice in an enclosed basalt frozen looking clumps or pockets of this water ice that we can hope to surface mine, trap, and process by heating slowly and thawing out, and then purifying and filtering the new water for our use.

Then after that we can chemically convert it to its base chemical element parts of oxygen and distilled water, and also then to make liquified hydrogen gas being reserved for our capsule shuttle pods excursion and our spacecraft rocket engines to take us back home to Earth in the future.

Our Triton Moon Scientist Astronauts are;
   a) **Franz Waldheim**, m Chief Triton Supervisor and Geologist
   b) **Paul Stewart**, Co-Pilot and Robotics specialist
   c) **Arlene Cummings**, f Wellness and Greenhouse Horticulturist
   d) **Jennifer Aldridge**, f Nuclear Physicist and System Engineer
   e) **Ramon Sanchez**, m Chief Plumber and thermal Electrician

    f)   **Peter Walker,** m Chief Chemist Hydrologist and Biologist
    g) **Mary Walton**, f Medical Doctor and Biologist, and Nutritionist
    h) **Anna Magdalena**, f Chief Pilot and Communications Officer
    i)   **Marcus Santora, m Chief demolition and Triton rover driver**

I) Daxor AI-5 Cyborg Robot, Chief human formed Android with three multifunction eyes, with thermal x-ray, a 200-core brain sized multi-processor running at 60-GHZ with twenty terabytes of on board programming read on AI memory and twenty teraflops of on board multi-system function core memory.

These eight Triton SHOPs are compartment designed and insulated from the extreme cold here on Triton's surface temperature in our cocoon POD laboratories or platforms along with our advanced geological laboratories sleeping quarters, greenhouse for food production and mess hall capability that are centrally powered by three medium portable thorium nuclear fusion reactor battery units in meeting our electrical and heating needs for our crew of eight a graviton wheel pod, and Daxor our cyborg assistant here, with our scientific long stay of almost ten years exploration and settlement expansion and base development here on this moon, Triton.

Eight POD Shops (Science Habitat operational Platforms)
    A) **SHOP (1), Sleeping Library and resting quarters**
    B) **SHOP (2), Mess hall and hospital infirmary**
    C) **SHOP (3), Geological facility**
    D) **SHOP (4), Chemical facility**
    E) **SHOP (5), Robotic communication and network computer**
    F) **SHOP (6), External drilling laboratory facility**
    G) **SHOP (7), Garden and greenhouse unit**
    H) **SHOP (8), Garage Nuclear power and exploratory vehicle center**
    M) **SHOP (9), Astronomy and Deep Space research unit**

I) Four (later six) Thorium AX5 reactors Nuclear electric batteries units.

J) Two external dish communication antennas

K) Three external multifunction telescope observation mounted units

L) Graviton rotating Wheel wellness and exercise unit Pod

Each Shop is connected by a twenty foot extension causeway tube that is an atmospheric mix and fully pressurized and insulated by the outside frigid elements in going from one SHOP Pod to another on this very cold Neptune surface moon.

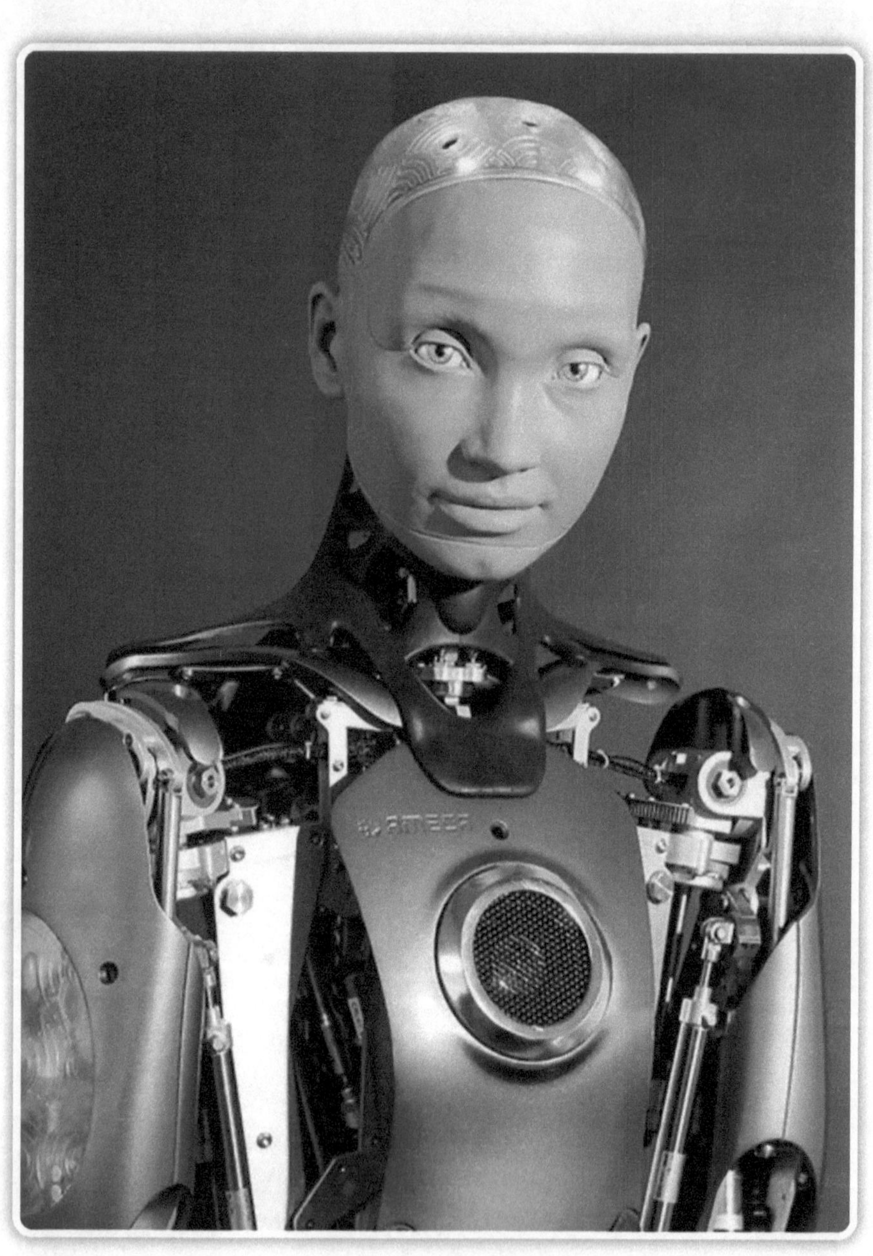

Again, my name is Astro-Chemical Geologist, **Franz Waldheim**, I am chief Supervisor here at Cosmoport, and my story deals with a strange encounter here on Triton. As I have said we have discovered from our orbiting spacecraft an almost one foot wide hole seeping frozen vapor of mostly frozen vapor of oxygen with carbon dioxide, nitrogen and methane mix gases escaping from this vent and that is when we decided to come here and land at this site after looking for a settlement base for one Earth time month here while coming from Earth in our orbit of Triton.

In selecting our new settlement base in our finding the right spot finally we noticed this slowly escaping gas somewhere in the cracked basalt rock which we could use to our advantage, as we mentioned before, we then setup this base and expanded it, and then our crew burrowed deep into this seeping vented hole about two feet wide from barely less than one foot wide in a newly made circumference hole, and with it going down to almost one hundred feet deep is where we found with our instruments these seeping gas coming from somewhere with our possible new means to extricate down there and then to expand our base by doing so we then encountered a strange phenomena and where our story truly begins now.

TRINEP 1-1, spacetime

We have sent down a robotic AI caterpillar in the new vented hole that we created with the caterpillar that is nine inches wide by six feet in length, with its high two million beam searchlights, life sensors, night scope cameras, and scooping up sampling analyzer capabilities so we can monitor up here on the surface the results and movement of the

AI caterpillar in this new subterranean underground world of no more than fifteen feet.

Our AI robotic caterpillar has landed on a completely dark black underground world that is only eight feet up to only a maximum of fifteen feet deep between frozen basalt rock ice ceiling and a frozen ice flooring that is the underground floor, and we have evaluated from the AI caterpillar that this is on a condensed frozen water ice and not that much granite rock or basalt like rock found on its vertical tunnel wall that we made in reaching this depth.

We allowed the caterpillar to go one hundred feet from the vertical tunnel hole, with its temperature reading of an incredible 38 degrees while everyone rejoiced at its findings that our Android Daxor is controlling it and our team monitoring the caterpillar's nighttime course above here at the surface finding so much ice appealing that has not turned into a hard granite ice mineral like the hard granite ice on the surface and now making us again here very happy that we found at least mush like soft ice here in abundant water form supply that we can transfer and melt into pure water and with it creating a large enough reservoir for our multiple needs here on Triton's surface.

But we are very intrigued about this find and our scientist, 'Peter Walker', now speculates that the deeper we go the more this ice will become soft cold water from its crystallized granite ice here at the surface and with another scientist, 'Arlene Cummings', said we have only to go between two and three hundred feet further down inside this moon Triton that will give us a larger water reservoir in the millions of gallons for centuries to come, and then said another scientist, 'Mary Walton' speculating the potential here is enormous, so now we have allowed the AI caterpillar ony one hundred feet leeway traveling on this mush soft water ice, and the AIC then detected to everyone again how constant in this warm atmosphere of only thirty eight degrees in this fifteen foot maximum subsurface underground world and in its comparison to the temperature on the very, very cold surface we are on.

The temperature down the new vent hole is only thirty eight degrees with our diamond industrial digging tool in reaching this depth of almost one hundred feet down in this basalt and granite condensed granite ice (nitrogen/hydrogen and oxygen with carbon monoxide atmospheric mix) wall and of this surface moon, and again our science team was completely surprised being that there was no change in its constant temperature around our new vertical hole in its underground surface where it is thirty eight degrees, reaching the ice bottom and we are very happy with our mining circular 2.2 foot very hard industrial diamond saw creating the vertical hole reaching this underground world.

With this great news here on the moon's surface where the temperature is a little under four hundred degrees minus zero Fahrenheit, that is what another scientist we call cold up here said to one scientist, 'Ramon Sanchez', remarked.

In the SHOP Pod no. 6 mining lab, chemist Peter Walker, also a geological chemist said that we have an opportunity to dig into the frozen bottom ice that is soft enough to bring up with its fast pressurized hydrogen and water mush that is heated by our intake nozzle to our purification and distillation units so we can sample out any microbes that could exist for our hygiene and food processing use among other uses.

The geological and chemical science team of 'Franz Waldheim, Peter Walker, Arlene Cummings', found that this miniature maximum fifteen foot underground world needs to be further explored with the three scientist and now coming on board 'Paul Stewart', sending another specialized robotic caterpillar down this time it will have another purpose and a much greater range of up to two miles from the vertical hole that we created and it can explore in this narrow 8 to 15 foot height ceiling world from the surface with our ability to create a three dimensional display soon on this second caterpillar sent down.

Now with the thermal hose pipe that 'Ramon Sanchez', workshop now is being crafted and then soon attaching it to the soft ice surface below that the first caterpillar found with its powerful mapping microwave radar attachment in sending us detailed data that this soft ice goes straight down well over two hundred feet.

Then the second caterpillar is now being lowered and measuring up to thirteen feet in length, it has a caterpillar multi-pod body sensors, with six communication and directional relay system pods, and also it has two floating and two submersible water like ball sensor pods that tests the purity, quality, temperature and electrical output of the liquid water it is in contact with among other sensor uses.

TRINEP, 2-1, spacetime

The second caterpillar has now traveled for fifteen minutes in complete darkness except for its powerful two million watt traveling flash beams creating a beautiful rainbow in this blue world underneath its granite ice ceiling and ice flooring at almost one hundred feet down from the 'Cosmoport", base vertical hole, with this second caterpillar now reaching over five hundred feet further on in this dark subterranean world now automatically deploying one of its four directional beacon mushroom pods, and then in just over five hundred feet from the vertical hole, thirty minutes later it stopped because in front of them is a seven hundred foot oval circular like round pond going down just barely five feet just beneath the standing caterpillar then launching the floating water ball instrument sensoring pod down on to this near frozen cold water pond and when it landed on the liquide water its temperature reading was an incredible 38-degrees fahrenheit similar to the atmospheric reading with the scientist crew now totally ecstatic and slightly baffled with one scientist speculated by the caterpillars results, that there is a liquid water world underneath Triton that the human race can use to explore further this outerworld moon in creating a settlement here at Cosmoport, for over one hundred people is now very possible here on Triton.

The scientists are now reading the data and photographic pictures of the miniature thirty two megapixel zoom pod camera on the caterpillar of this crystal blue water world with no impurities or parasites or bacteria of any kind in its water by its sensors, they could hardly believe it that there is water plenty down there but no life in it for now, they question the data and finds that we have to believe what it says and Daxor confirming its results to the others present, with all here present that at least we have water from now on and that is the main thing going for us here right now, they all agreed, and now the science team deployed a second mushroom pod, but this one acts like a submersible like submarine in it diving a mere fifty feet down and stabilizing, and hoping in collecting the same data as the floating mushroom pod has.

The submersible pod now deployed has gone down fifty feet in the water and now it reads a fifty two degree water temperature down below the surface water line and then one scientist, 'Peter Walker', said there has to be an active hot liquid core inside this moon, and then the robotic android Daxor cyborg said for now we have to conclude that very real theory.

TRINEP 3-1 spacetime

While one scientist are watching their viewing screens and data terminal computers and instrument panels regarding caterpillar findings, up at thirty two thousand feet in Triton orbit the artificially intelligent computer from the Venture spaceship has detected a very mild and weak signal coming from one thousand miles northeast from the Cosmoport settlement location site and then the Venture, spacecraft AI on board network computer then signals that to the Cosmoport,,

SHOP, number 5 communications unit its warning and letting the astronaut scientists know of the direction of the signal.

The chief astronaut and communications officer that is second in command here on Triton, Anna Magdalena, has said while Franz Waldheim, now chief administrator of this Triton base, Cosmoport, concentrates on our water survival find deep below our surface, she and Paul Stewart and Daxor cyborg robot will investigate this weak signal coming from one thousand miles northeast from Cosmoport, base then the two of them and the cyborg will be in full communication with Cosmoport, and you Franz Waldheim,

Then Franz Waldiem, in saying good luck in your search to Anna, Paul, and Daxor, and she retorted back to him thank you Franz and, if we get into any trouble we will call and communicate with you immediately from the signal. Then the three of them left Pod 6 (Anna, Paul with Daxor) and then went to Pod no.5 communications and they carefully increases and modifies the amplification of the transmission being sent to the orbiting spaceship Venture, and its AI relayed back to the main SHOP 5 pod unit the constant message while listening on its repeating alien broadcast over and over again, with Daxor saying to Anna and Paul that their on board battery device must be running out of power according to the Venture AI program and Anna saying to them we will now have to go to this beacon's origin.

The orbiting spacecraft Venture now fully in remote control by Daxor cyborg through the spacecraft on board network computer will now be directed by its remote control through the Daxor AI two way built-in terminal relay into the SHOP 5 communications systems and will now send to the spacecraft Venture, overhead to the incoming weak signal one thousand miles away,

In the meantime at the Cosmoport hanger lies two of our four seater capsules ascend and lander pods and bringing the one pod down to number 2 transport pad ready to move, the three of them got into the capsule pod shuttle checking all its systems for a go and then after five minutes, now the moving transport pad and capsule shuttle pod has moved to the outside surface launch pad ready to launch and then go to the northeast location with the three of them now finally lifting off and with its four main engines launches and accelerates upward to a cruising speed at two hundred and sixty miles per hour in getting there in just over three Earth hours later and with Daxor cyborg robot directing the Venture, to analyze and decode the signal in what it means when the shuttle pod finally arrives over the alien spacecraft with the Venture, spacecraft overhead at thirty two thousand miles above making sure it safe to land on the spacecraft.

With Paul Stewart, Anna Magdalena, and Daxor cyborg robot arriving there while the Venture, has reached its robotic controlled destination high above the alien spacecraft where it is now analyzing and taking measurements of the alien spacecraft with the capsule pod that has now safely landed on its upper surface hull, now inside the capsule shuttle pod the three of them communicating through Daxor cyborg to the Venture spacecraft have found it to be 95 % submerged into the thick nitrogen and methane near petrified condensed snow with only a small sliver of this estimated three hundred foot diameter round spacecraft upper surface hull exposed and with a near eighty-five foot depth, Daxor receiving information from the Venture, spacecraft above has found an entrance way hatch door we can use quite nearby next to the landed capsule shuttle pod.

Now safely landed on top of the upper hull of the alien spacecraft the three of them went out onto the slippery cold surface hull, while now walking gently they came upon what Daxor believed to be a hatch door and to its right side is a small oval panel that could open the hatch door for us, and with Daxor x-ray optical eye has indeed determined that this is the way we should enter the spaceship, now in communicating through their helmets in their special space suits to Anna and Paul. Then Daxor said to Paul can I use your battery rechargeable unit laying on your right side, and he said yes then giving it to Daxor, and then the cyborg robot taking the unit and placing it on top of the panel fixture with safety features off and with Anna Magdalena watching and then she said to Daxor cyborg via helmet intercon that we better get inside in less than twenty minutes or we will abort and go back to the capsule shuttle pod, due to the extreme cold weather outside here and our spacesuits not been able to keep us warm for too long.

Daxor with his two fingers now exposed to the elements and then with a small electric pulse sent through his two finger hand an electric power current surge has created into the unsafe mode rechargeable unit creating a two hundred watt spark on to the fixture panel then waiting thirty seconds later the upper hull door hatch opened up and sending an elevator platform up to the hatch door reaching them, now the three of them quickly went inside and onto the platform elevator and with Daxor opening up his palm sent a universal code command to the elevator platform now sending them down into the spaceship while also closing the hatch door behind them.

The three of them went down inside the elevator platform with their electromagnetic impulse static revolvers set at stung mode and with Daxor opening up his palm hand again sent a universal code command to the platform elevator to take us to the next available floor going down inside the alien spaceship, now completely dark they opened up their high beam flashlights now looking intensely and somewhat frightened going down inside the spaceship then the door on this floor opened up and getting off they noticed a rounded hallway and then walking on it and following it they reached what they believe to be the bridge and looking around they noticed what could be a power on button and pressing it the entire spaceship systems came on including its thermal heating unit that was needed while it was only slightly warmer than on the outside and then they noticed these sitting on their command console post seats were six dead frozen alien corpse looking a bit like modified six foot reptiles with a red pink peach color hue skin all now frozen dead with Paul finding the 'may day' echo beacon on and then he noticed it could be on its very last battery legs of power he then turned it off with Daxor confirming his results that this spaceship has been here a very long time, perhaps decades.

Daxor looking at these console panels noticed there were several nine by seven inch touch pads around them and opening his hand from his spacesuit he held his hand three inches above the touchpads and then with his cyborg computer brain interfaced with the alien database computer system and Daxor said to Anna and Paul I will be here a little while gaining whatever information I can obtain.

Now leaving the bridge Anna and Paul walked around the hallway and came upon the cryogenics stasis chamber beds and Anna counting the beds she said to paul there are eighteen empty beds here with Paul saying to her where the other twelve aliens go, and Anna said perhaps they somehow left the saucer looking for food or even water below this moon, and then a few minutes later noticed that Daxor has not returned to them and Paul said he may still be at the bridge looking at their consoles databases, then two minutes later Daxor came into the stasis chamber and Anna said to him did you complete your computer interface with this alien computer system and Daxor said yes, then please stay close and we cannot lose each other here on the spaceship and Daxor complied with her wishes.

Paul then said to her and Daxor let's go down one floor and look around for more clues and then Daxor noticed an elevator like transport chute device just outside the stasis chamber and the three of them went down to the one floor below and found that these aliens went exploring inside the moon similar to us and then they noticed that the makeshift vertical tunnel well that was created was five feet wide and aiming their two million watt high beam flashlights they could not reach the bottom, this hole must be very deep, Paul said.

Now looking around they noticed six hovercraft scooter like machines with Anna asking Paul we may have to come back here tomorrow and explore here more with Anna and Paul and Daxor taking high definition videos and still pictures of their encounter here and one more on the bridge with Anna, Paul and Daxor looking now again at these alien pilots dead frozen corpses and then they went to the elevator platform and left for the surface and leaving the round hatch doorway with Daxor looking back at the panel mechanism with his eyes and two fingers electronically diagnosis the unit and carefully walks back to their capsule shuttle pod and then they took off for their settlement base, Cosmoport.

Franz Waldiem and his crew are still exploring the subterranean world with the second caterpillar now going and reaching at five hundred feet from their SHOP vertical no. 6 hole and this time they explored a small near oval round seven hundred foot wide water ice pond that is only five feet down below from the rock ice bank surface of this eight by fifteen foot dark black subterranean world, when then their second caterpillar read 35 degrees at this oval lake surface temperature and now the second caterpillar has launched its underwater submersible pod with it going down fifty feet below the pond's water surface line and it read this water depth temperature to be 52 degrees fahrenheit. They all looked at each other and with all smiles and congradulations thanked each other for this great find for our new settlement base here on Triton has begun for us.

The submersible pod is only designed to hover at fifty feet below the surface and there is still plenty of water going down further below the pod. Franz Waldheim said to the other's present this pond must be a large vent going very deep and later we find how deep it really is in reaching over three hundred feet down, for now we are very rich in water resources here, now we have to tap it for our growing needs and use at Cosmoport, and I believe we have our six hundred foot special intake hose that will do the job fine.

As they were about to sign off for the day the second caterpillar submersible detected through its underwater pod an electrical discharge in the deep part of the water vent coming slowly up to the near surface about seventy feet below the submersible pod that has measured it to be 1400 volts, then all of a sudden it disappeared going back down with no trace reading of any new discharge at all, the scientific crew reacting to this anomaly could not explain this electrical discharge emanating in the deep water vent, now fifteen minutes went by and nothing has happened again they then signed off and Franz Waldheim said we will start over again in the morning, for now we can bring up the submersible pod to the surface and have the caterpillar pick it up with its grappling hook line and let it stay there until we can start over again in the later morning here on Triton.

At the settlement base, Cosmoport, later that 3-1 spacetime, there was a meeting at the conference/mess hall table where Anna Magdalena and Franz Waldheim called a special meeting to discuss what they experienced the last twenty four Earth hours, Anna and Paul discussing with the group of their travel and exploration of the alien saucer spacecraft and just recently Franz 0Waldiem discussing Their anomaly down in the small oval lake.

Franz Waldheim,
Question; first we will hear from Anna Magdalena regarding the alien spacecraft and their findings.
Answer; we have a chance to further explore this strange alien saucer.

Paul Stewart,
Question; the alien saucer is quite advanced but where are the aliens?
Answer; only by going back to the saucer will we ever know what happened.

Arlene Cummings,
Question; the findings down below are outstanding but for this anomaly
Answer; when we go down there again we use caterpillar III robot diver.

Jennifer Aldridge,
Question greenhouse and biological anomalies in food production.
Answer yes you are quite right and it took three hours to correct.

Ramon Sanchez,
Question anomalies regarding heat and proper ventilation at cosmoport
Answer yes heating and oxygen levels disruption from time to time.

Peter Walker,
Question disturbances involving hydrogen and chemical separations
with certain sectors of cosmoport
Answer yes these sectors had low oxygen levels and insufficient lab
work.

Mary Walton,
Question Any discrepancies with patient stats in readings and diagnosis
Answer My readings were way off and the medical computer showed
wrong results every time where I had to constantly recalibrate my
readings

Anna Magdalena,
Question Any discrepancies with Earth communication
Answer yes my computer logging and directional finding at times
could not point to Earth, instead only showing mars or the asteroid
belt, in which I had to correct the gyroscopic navigation unit positions
of the antennas to adjust to Earth's position as opposed to ours here
on Triton.

Daxor cyborg robot,
discusses his thoughts on the alien spacecraft, my program from this
time needs recalibration I fear there is an enemy program trying to
disrupt my robotic AI system and I am constantly reprogramming my
systems memory functions. With the alien space craft we need to go
back and explore more.

They all were giving their opinions and conclusions of their stay on Triton's moon so far to date. Then Franz Waldheim said to the others do not repeat or send any information about this to Earth Space Command and keep on building this settlement base here on Triton and they all agreed to do that.

TRINEP 4-1, spacetime

On Triton's moon, at their now usual Cosmoport, breakfast meeting Mark Walheim again discussed 3-1 spacetime, meeting and in our belief that this alien spacecraft lying there in this methane nitrogen frozen gas has been there a very long time possibly over one hundred years dormant except for an occasional distress signal that appears to be as of now by Daxor running out of a century old battery life and that is why it was best to turn it off, but as a result we will not utilize the second caterpillar today. Instead now we will concentrate on the alien spacecraft now, Ann9a, Paul, Ramon and Myself will go to the spacecraft with Daxor's created remote control given to us that will open the hatch door and will also control the elevator platform to take us down inside the spacecraft with Daxor saying there is enough voltage in its main power units for us to go inside the spaceship to have heat and light, and for a full system power up of no more than sixty Earth minutes, now in thirty minutes us four will be going there so please finish up your breakfast and prepare to leave here for that alien spacecraft with the rest of our crew will monitor our findings in SHOP no. 5 and thank you team for your cooperation, and in 29 minutes we go.

In Just under four hours they arrived at the coordinate site beneath the high altitude 'Venture, orbiting spacecraft. They stepped out of the capsule shuttle pod and carefully walking over to the hatch doorway they put the remote device near to the side of the panel unit and it opened with the elevator platform coming up and the four scientists went in and went down closing the hatch door behind them.

Once inside the alien spacecraft they went first to the bridge and then with Daxor schematics went down to the engine room and Ramon looking at its power drive system said this is quite advanced but I believe I could repair it with no problem, fine said Franz Waldheim you can reach us by our communicators because we are going to their mining chamber.

At the mining chamber Mark Walheim was impressed of how they could create a five foot wide hole going extremely deep into this moon. And then he took out his carrying case of a flying drone and setting it up took three minutes and was now ready to fly down the hole and investigate what happened or is happening down there. In the meantime Anna went to the infirmary and into the bridge afterwards and to put together by herself their history and who they are in coming here to this moon.

At the infirmary she was impressed and horrified at what she saw, not only was their gruesome details about who they are with six dead bodies completely cut up and put into jars she believes to be eaten not diagnosis, but also she found dead salamander like electric eel creatures with their bodies petrified and made into natural producing electric batteries, there must have been hundreds of these thirteen foot creatures in there very tall jars like holding pens except for the one jar that was empty of its contents, and with the petrified rest present their with something like wired cords penetrating from their dead bodies leading up to the ceiling.and perhaps going to the spacecraft power units then looking around further she found a door and pressed its opening button and inside was laboratory with these creatures in several display modes of development with one of these creatures still alive barely and what looks like very soon it will give birth, in front of the holding vessel this creature are several buttons and his touchpad on and one of them was something like a red button key with a turn of touch button representing death and she then pressed it and then all of a sudden the creature violently shook looking at her and then turned petrified and electrocuting her eggs she was going to produce and killing them instantly and turning this light green and pink with black striping creature all petrified and solid black.

When she arrived at the bridge later she got into their historical database that Daxor provided for her with their password entry key and then she went through their history and looking over two hundred years ago their mothership was about to enter a small black hole when unable to escape its gravitational pull they had to escape and eject themselves like a life buoy in the ocean on Earth, according to their files only fifteen of these life buoy's escaped their mothership that within moments later was engulfed and consumed by this black hole and this particular spacecraft took many years in space until it decided to hitch itself a ride on an asteroid from the Kuiper belt and finally freeing itself from its grasp it landed here about one hundred years ago on this ice world,Triton.

Then trying to stay alive they then consumed these salamander electric eel like animals when they eventually depleted without a proper feeding diet slowly they turned to a savage cannibalism eating their own and then their spaceship which eventually was covered by snow of nitrogen and methane. They sent out their last mayday signal hoping their fellow aliens could somehow find them and then before they died...it ends here with Anna Magdalena saying to herself we should just let this spaceship stay here in memoriam and not to disturb it any further.

Franz Waldheim walked inside the bridge with Ramon and Paul carrying a mining round circular cutting five foot multi width blade for our enlarging the hole from two feet to our new five feet width where now we can for ourselves go down in this new five foot wide vertical tunnel hole to this one hundred foot subterranean world, and he said to her that Ramon agreeing that he thought he could fix the main drive propulsion unit but it is too far gone and I'm afraid this alien spaceship is here to stay inside this frozen gases petrified condensed mixture and Franz Waldheim said we have brought with us their weapons and mobile communicators that even now seem advanced to us, and we must go now back to Cosmoport, and then they all left to go up the elevator platform just barely able to carry the round circular five foot cutting blade with us four being careful not to cut ourselves in it to the surface hatch and once up there they got into their capsule shuttle pod loading the circular cutting blade carefully into their holding compartment and then they took off for their home base with Franz communicating with Daxor requesting him to return the Venture, spaceship to our Cosmoport, coordinance over at our settlement base and he said that he will do as you instructed as of now.

Back four hours later, Franz Waldheim had a brief meeting with everyone in attendance and said to them the drone that I sent down at one thousand feet saw nothing but pure pristine water with one exception the water is one hundred and sixty five degrees fahrenheit and what a sight it is to behold for the water measures well over two thousand square feet in a triangle shape and possibly quite deep, and with this news that the interior core of this moon is indeed hot with a possible molten core underneath in providing heat, and for us that is great news for we can now have a small colony settlement here on Triton and we will discuss with Earth Space Command to allow us to send additional housing and equipment here to Triton for a more detailed colony and observation of Pluto and Charon and also the Kuiper belt in the near future through Venture, orbiting spacecraft that still has it dish and high resolution telescope on board.

TRINEP 5-1, spacetime

---

they all continued their work on the small pond, now sending two robotic walking assembly sticks down to attach a piping hose and place its intake nozzle just twenty feet down its water surface line from the ice surface, and to secure it for our water needs for at our surface SHOP's in where we can now shower, cook food and utilize water in our own SHOP labs.

On Triton in SHOP no. 7 Greenhous Pod is arlene Cummings and Daxor the cyborg robot now perfecting their hydroponic garden planting of the typical but genetically modified food bulb stock and then tweaking the protons and proteins into its new conversion food processing matrix machine unit and creating the perfect animal like taste of roast beef that cannot be distinguished from the real thing that they have on Earth where arlene and Daxor will present it to the mess hall with the other scientist astronauts providing a taste test.

When out of nowhere an emergency siren alarm rings throughout the Cosmoport, pod base colony, and it was coming from SHOP Pod no. 6 where Franx Waldheim and Paul Stewart just fended off an incredible creature presumed to be thirteen foot long came up climbing the water intake hose and coming up onto the ice surface near the no.2 second caterpillar where the Caterpillar through commands from above took evasive moves and thwarting its attempt to destroy the second Caterpillar now with red, white, and blue strobe lighting of two million lumens in its face then the second Caterpillar took several flashlight pictures of this assault and then the second caterpillar blared loud siren blasting sounds at it and then the salamander electric-eel looking creature decided to retreat and went back into the water with the caterpillar lights flashing red, blue and green at the creature leaving the second Caterpillar alone.

Then Mark Waldheim looking at these pictures agreed with the robotic Caterpillar that the creature is believed to be thirteen feet long emitting its own electric flashing show to the Caterpillar that recorded its wattage to be 1400 volts. Franz Waldheim looking at the Caterpillar video and high definition pictures asked the scientific crew is this the only creature here on Triton or are there more waiting for us somewhere near here, the SHOP crew members could not answer him and Franz

Waldheim said in thirty minutes there will be a meeting in the mess hall for questions and answers to be handed out and taken.

Now everyone present at the mess hall meeting Franz Waldheim wants answers as to what is this creature and does anybody know of it and Anna Magdalena answered Franz Waldheim and said to him and to the others that while I was in the infirmary like lab inside the alien spacecraft I came along this empty vessel jar with nothing to indicate it had a dead corpse body in it, from what you are telling me and us is that creature is somehow alive and is now in this underground pond, yes I am telling you that and how it got there I do not know but more important how is it able to stay alive with what food source is it getting it from, again I do not know, and I believe this creature could be very similar to a microscopic targrasse animal with incredible staying alive properties that has existed for a very, very long time here on Triton.

TRINEP 6-1, spacetime

The early morning spacetime Franz Waldheim called everybody to the mess hall and when they arrived Mark Waldheim announced very bad news that the alien spaceship has now just self destructed with a shock wave and explosion extending over two hundred miles from the alien spaceship in completely gone and here are the video pictures from Venture, showing the massive explosion on the grounded spaceship with everyone here are completely shocked and truly surprised with Anna Magdalena asking what happened and Daxor may have given the answer that when we and I was at the panel unit it may have triggered their self destruct countdown procedure that was installed by the aliens, luckily twice we did not stay long or attempted to go back there, for if we did we too would have died in the explosion by our simple curiosity.

Then with the hose and cable lines removed and reeled up to the Shop no.6 pod, Franz Waldheim and Paul Stewart and Ramon Sanchez in

SHOP no. 6 drilling Pod carefully installed their new five foot circular drilling unit on to their motorized machine and then Ramon turning on the machine now circulating and going down into the two foot hole is slowly is now working going down one hundred feet or every ten feet expanded hole cut is one hour and ten minutes cutting time, or in just under twelve hours the mining expansion will be completed with a five foot fine smooth wall that will take us to this subterranean underground world and we can see for ourselves what it's like there.

Now just under thirteen hours they finished the width expansion of the vertical tunnel hole and now with enough room the scientific crew of Franz Waldheim, Paul Stewart and Arlene Cummings is suiting up in their special mechanized one hundred foot created rope harness and now with Franz Waldheim went first and is self lowered down ten stories on to this frozen subterranean ice world, the process took no more than ten minutes and next in line is Peter Stewart, and last is Arlene Cummings reaching the ice ground floor and Ramon Sanchez and now Anna Madalena are looking at the screens and monitoring them on the mining wall display in SHOP no. 6 Pod.

They are using their extreme two million watt flashlight high beams and their mining hat also with its high beam attached to it and now walking up to the first caterpillar and then moving on to the second caterpillar and the pond they simply followed the piping hose and now reaching the pond looked at it with their high beam lights and the fifteen foot ceiling of rock and ice that is thirty two degrees on our mobile gauge computer temperature tablet console unit with Ramon and Anna continuously speaking and monitoring them while it is complete darkness except for their high beam searchlights.

Mary Walton of the SHOP no.2 infirmary said to by video intercom to Daxor cyborg robot and Anna Magdalena that I have looked at the video and documents you two have presented to our network library database in regard to this creature resembling a mix of a salamander and an electric eel with its ability to walk up ice sheets wall with its eight suction cup like limb legs.

And, I have just figured out a way to neutralize the creature and I have contacted Ramon Sanchez to build this weapon with the available tools and equipment we have here and he said he will build it and present it to you in two Triton Neptune day times, meanwhile down below in this sunrerrarian fifteen foot ceiling world Franz Waldheim with is high beam flashlight looked down into the twenty foot down water line surface crystal clear bluish water and saw this creature creating its own bio-lumenance to navigate the dark blackness of this underground world and he thought this creature was somehow lost and seemed quite lonely swimming by itself fifty to seventy feet down inside the water.

Then Franz Waldheim, Paul, and Arlene decided to walk another seven hundred feet and discovered a much larger pond resembling a small lake also pure with no impurities and completely fresh unspoiled looking seeing this lake is completely to them being surprised of the amount of clear bluish lighted with their high beams shining on the frozen water surface with its top oxygen and nitrogen layer mix here on the five foot down ice crystal shore line where they analyzed it on their tablet of this frozen top lake composition, with only twelve hundred feet walking distance from the new five wide vertical hole that we have created.

While Waldheim and Arlene were at this lake, Paul Stewart decided to walk further on and noticed after what he thought was a thousand feet where the walls of this subterranean world and simply walking and thinking about this moon, in this complete darkness, while walking with his cane in guiding him all of a sudden there was no ground ice and he stopped putting on in his helmet the night scope of two thousand lumens video helmet display and putting his high beam flashlight on its hi-point setting saw something that is frightening and awesome, he was standing on this ice ledge with his high beams and he calls this the grand canyon underground world on Triton aiming his high beams going down what he estimates to be over thirty stories down and perhaps left one mile wide by two miles in length.

And, in the middle of this canyon is a moving river that is free flowing and not frozen at all. Then he looked up and the ceiling became over one hundred feet throughout this canyon, Excited, he then contacted Franz Waldheim and Arlene to come over quickly and they did and when they came they were completely flabbergasted and in complete awe. They then took whatever night scope pictures they could and then after a few minutes they left to go back up the vertical hole and to their SHOP Pods for another meeting of today's subterranean sojourn travels. At the meeting they saw the video and still pictures on their wall seventy inch display,and the crew was equally amazed and was incredible awe and that is why we are very glad we are here, said Anna Magdalena.

Mary Walton, interject the meeting and said looking at the video display said to the crew what is that moving lights in the river on the canyon bottom. Then Paul said back to Mary that is my high beam two flashlights looking down on to that river and then Daxor cyborg robot looking at the video pictures said no that is not the high beam flashlight, and Paul said to Daxor what do you mean, Daxor said, that light being emitted is multicolored is actually six different lights and bioluminescence also, and not the pure white light emitted by your high beam flashlights they then all looked again at the repeated video and Franz Walheim said to Daxor you are completely right. Then Franz Waldheim said these creatures seen three hundred feet in the river in this small canyon a couple days ago, while one of them was up here in this lake then I believe this lake must go down at least three hundred feet below and connecting to that river and now we see these creatures down in that river and my question to all of you here is where does that river go to and then Anna Magdalena said perhaps it goes all the way up to where the alien spacecraft was trapped in the permafrost crystalline snow field covering, and then everyone said back to her that is a good possibility.

The next three scientist of Ramon Sanchez, Peter Walker, and Mary Walton working together created out of their reserve secondary space suits simplified these suits making it more comfortable to move around in for their expanded Pod work and in converting the subterranean world more easily and putting a couple of conversion atmospheric converters down below into the new housed modules in placing these specialized pumping equipment and sending the fresh oxygen mix and also to send the fresh water from the pond to the Pod filter machines up on the surface for our SHOP needs and survival and then later that day which has become nighttime on Triton in the SHOP no. 1 resting community room Pod, there was a small fashion show where Mary Walton handed out the nine modified 'Triton' suits with everyone very happy with them and now we can move around more comfortably in our work on this moon.

Now at their breakfast in the mess hall there was a radio signal from Earth that there will be a factory ship coming your way. they are sending another factory ship the radio broadcast has confirmed and will arrive at your Triton orbit in two of our Earth days time on board it will replenish all your requirement needs for the next five years and on board their are two scientist astronauts one is a specialized medical genetics doctor and one is an astrophysicist astronomer in which we are sending you a powerful telescope that will look deep inside the Kuiper belt, and the one medical officer will now compliment your doctor, Mary Walton and your biologist, Peter Walker.

10) **Laura Philmore** f, Genetic Medical Biologist and Doctor
11) **Jackson Banes** m, Astrophysicist and astronomer

For now we will send you the beginning construction parts of a large greenhouse and a new medical extension unit Pod with a polyvinyl swimming pool and sun tanning lights spa with a jacuzzi for your recreation and comfort and also we will upgrade your new network computer that will last you for at least ten Earth yea's and we will give you upgrade systems function and memory for Daxor cyborg robot, and will have Franz Waldheim to oversee this new expansion of your SHOP pod Cosmoport, settlement base, and we now thank you for your service on Neptune's moon Triton.

From our Earth Space planetary Outerworld Command, (ESPOC) that is all and now we will end our dish communication transmission from Earth.

Franz Waldheim said to everyone at our 2-2 spacetime, tomorrow we have a lot of work to do in receiving from the Factory spaceship our new shipments and we will then speed up and expedite the transfer from space to Triton surface and in giving them detailed geographic information to the soon to be orbiting spaceship and its two crewmen where to place the Pod's and the merchandise equipment and secondary units for our settlement expansion item logistics on this ground and then greet our new two guests as they will be part of our new team here on Triton.

TRINEP 2-2, spacetime

It is now on Triton later, and the factory ship has just arrived in orbit around Triton and Franz Waldheim is now coordinating with robotic remote control by Daxor cyborg in interfacing with Cosmoport, and the Venture, network computer and the factory ship's network computer systems to bring down the factory ship pods, and selected on board items and placing it on the ground right next to the Cosmoport, base with the crew members of Anna Magdalena and Ramon Sanchez have already taken two space shuttle pods selected immediate items from the Factory ship along with their two passengers of Laura Philmore, Jackson Banes, down to Cosmoport, base and are now coordinating also the landing operations at the settlement base for the rest of its shipments and are now emptying out the factory ship and only leaving there two thorium nuclear engines behind on board and now Anna Magdalena has put the factory ship to one hundred thousand miles above Triton along with the first factory ship that is stationed at eighty thousand miles located just five thousand miles apart and 'Cosmoport controlling its two orbits and making sure that their orbits does not decay within the ten years before unfortunately sending their two space factory ships to the surface of Triton in a massive explosion.

During the next three:

TRINEP 3-2, / 4-2/ 5-2

Spacetime days here on Triton they will start to complete their expansion and reorganized their settlement Cantaloupe mountain hill base in completing their new telescope and getting back really excellent pictures in finding several new wayward moons and asteroids in the Kuiper belt and showing very clear pluto and charon images as well as getting back new findings about these two worlds up close about almost one billion miles further from Triton.

TRINEP 3-2, spacetime

Our Cosmoport, base here has truly expanded. We are making this outpost base extremely user friendly and with our resupply by the second freighter we now have doubled the size of our greenhouse garden SHOP Pod no. 7 to produce our greater supply of vegetables and fruits, and with some of them converting them to other foods, like vegetable ground meat substitute. The great work done by our team, Laura Philmore, Alene Cummings, and Mary Walton in this lab extension to the greenhouse has provided varied food and proper nutrition for the ten people on Triton. Paul Stewart, Jennifer Aldridge, and Ramon Sanchez (who is also chief Machinist and Technology specialist), all three of them in an expanded SHOP Pod no. 8 Garage workshop units have created a specialized munitions jet propelled bullet that will neutralized and short circuit the creatures electrical system and also will automatically by doing so electrocute the creature from inside their bodies hopefully killing the creature..

Mark Waldheim said to SHOP no. 5 unit with Paul Stewart, Anna Magdalena, and Daxon the cyborg robot, have been given immediate instructions by Earth Space Command radio communications to me that we have to send the last freighter we sent to you (keeping the first freighter as backup) and to send it to Pluto, with its on board both radio dish antenna and on board telescopes that will communicate its results to the orbiting Venture, spacecraft and then to resend the information to Cosmoport and we will here explore and analyzing the sub-planet Pluto surface with only one billion miles separating us we will then process this new information provided there and relay this data back to Earth.

Down below one hundred feet, Franz Waldheim and Peter Walker are down in this subterranean world and are now fully exploring this dark world spending one to two hours in walking over two thousand feet on this cold frozen ice flooring and shining their high beam searchlights on the floor and ceiling shown this world completely basalt rock and ice giving it a rainbow with a blue hue everywhere on this other side of the small canyon where Paul walker speaking to Franz Waldheim saying I think we're on a plateau like surface terrace in this subterranean world and Franz Waldheim agreeing fully in saying yes and now realizing that this world is closing up on them and its ceiling becoming less than six feet and then they encountered nothing but a wall and following it five hundred feet and all of a sudden they encountered a ravine coming out of the wall going down over fifty feet by this terrace coming out of this wall now leveling off and then widening up to sixty feet down and fifty feet out from this wall then the revene then sunk down over two hundred feet and then they came around the ravine to the other side of this plateau like terrace near the seven hundred foot oval round pond looking like a volcano water filled vent and then their path lead them to the widening of this now fifteen foot subterranean world and now walking further it has become part of a widening terrace and canyon and the flowing river down below three hundred feet down.

Back on the surface and SHOP no. 5 communications and also the chief dish array and telescope control center where Daxor cyborg robot has detected an alien message from Pluto that has the same signature as the alien saucer spaceship a Triton days ago and it has the same 'mayday' help recording and now the last freighter we renamed 'searcher', that is already at two hundred miles from Triton, and headed for Pluto and will arrive at Pluto orbits in six Earth days or one Triton day from now said Daxor to Anna Magdalena and Paul Stewart, Daxor said to the other scientist I would like to take the first freighter and pilot the vessel at twenty thousand feet a map and explore the entire moon and this sojourner would only last one Triton day, Anna Magdalena said I would ask Franz Waldheim and Paul Walker when they come up from exploring the subterranean world in one Earth day and if they agree Daxor you may go up with one of our capsule shuttle pods and we will try best to monitor your circular low orbit of the moon.

It is three Earth hours later and at the mess hall with everyone eating their fresh greenhouse produced food, Daxor said to others sitting at the mess hall table that we need to explore and map these dark zones and what can we find just two thousand miles inside this dark zone of this cantaloupe moon if there are any tall mountains or deep ravine like canyons and before Daxor could say another word, Franz Waldheim said to Daxor go ahead you have my blessing and okay to proceed with your mission and good luck on your trip, and Daxor said are you sure and how did you know of my plan, and Franz Waldheim said, Anna Magdalena told me an hour ago of your plan to investigate and mapping and thought that is an excellent idea and this could be very useful for us as to what kind of moon we have here. And, then Daxor thanked

Franz Waldheim and said tomorrow I will begin at Earth time 0700 hours I will take off for the first 'freighter' I will rename, 'Meridien', and they all agreed your freighter we will called, 'meridien'.

TRINEP 4-2, spacetime

Daxor going to SHOP no. 8 garage said goodbye to Franz Waldheim and Anna Magdalena, until we meet again then boarded the space shuttle pod no. 2 and took off for the newly renamed freighter, 'meridien' spacecraft orbiting Triton. On board he established immediate communications with SHOP no.5 communications unit, and then turned on the spaceships systems ready launch diagnostic command and making sure the former freighter is ready to go and the on board computer said to Daxor all systems ready for a go. He then engaged and fired the thruster engines moving the spaceship, and then the spaceship went and left its parking orbit and then it went to an orbit of twenty five thousand feet and now traveling at less than one hundred miles per hour. Daxor then turned on the digital recording thirty megapixel high resolution three dimensional imaging mapping radar, and six 200-500 mm zoom, digital 30 megapixel 2000 lumens night scope cameras. The trip will take two Earth days north to south, and two Earth days east to west. While moving within an altitude of fifteen thousand to twenty five thousand feet in this now complete dark zone, that is not lighted at all by Neptune or far away sun.

While Daxor is on his mapping of Triton, down here at SHOP no. 6 mining unit and here with Franz Waldheim, Peter Walker and Mary Walton looking at their Pod screens of the underground subterranean world standing camera fixtures looking at the seven hundred foot oval round pond then there was a slight ripple in the cold water and coming out of this without warning were three salamander electric eels, that came out to its surface and then Paul Walker then put the standing twenty lights on strobe setting and the three came out in looking around staying a little while, when Franz Waldheim speaking to Peter Walker and said to him put on your harness gear equipment on and get these special guns with its rocket bullets, and then quickly in less than five minutes they put on their specialized suits and harness equipment and then they went down the vertical hole to the subterranean ice floor world below.

When they landed they took out their weapons and then these creatures came towards them and the vertical hole and they were now seen to be thirteen feet long with their five inch teeth and electrical sparks coming out of their mouths tongue and now attacking the two scientist and ready to be quickly consumed by the three of them when Franz and Paul fired and shot the three creatures in their mouths and sure enough they sensing their death left and went towards the pond and the three of them jumped into and dove down into the water and then the security cameras looking down at the water saw these creatures turn petrified black as they sinking down this volcano vent three hundred foot depth water pond.

Now Daxor cyborg robot with his artificial intelligence has now fully interfaced with the renamed ship, 'meridien', and is now flying over an extremely smooth area of Triton surface and when the ships special deep penetrating radar has detected that this surface is extreme frozen water ice underneath extreme frozen nitrogen and trace amounts of methane gas and carbon dioxide over this snow top layered frozen ocean, with the radar going down over Triton six hundred foot ocean with spot amounts of basalt ice rock islands. The area of this ocean is massive and Daxor believes it covers well over 45% of this moon surface. Traveling for a while the 'meridien'spaceship is flying over a two thousand five hundred mile island with a volcano mountain height of almost five thousand feet.

And, now flying directly overhead as it looks down on a volcano vent that is extremely covered with frozen mostly nitrogen and and some ice water with very little carbon monoxide vapors and below that down over one thousand feet where Daxor video camera showing thermal high resolution displays and sees a temperature of over two hundred degrees fahrenheit with Daxor confirming that there is a hot molten core of some kind in the center of Triton and coming up this vent to below one thousand feet before the extreme cold of this moon keeps it hidden and protected and cooling it as it rises to the volcano external rim where it meets the outside elements on its surface and now going past this island he sees the horizon is now completely empty of islands with an extremely smooth frozen surface of nitrogen with underneath frozen ice water ocean and then his ship the 'meridien', deep penetrating radar then picks up an ocean depth of over three hundred feet to its bottom with this imaging radar determining this underwater feature looks more like a chasm or a canyon going for over two thousand miles in the distance or one fifth the size of this frozen ocean.

Then traveling five Earth hours he then notices the forward thermal screen what he believes is the other side of Triton where the ocean meets the continent and approaching this other side of Triton then notices something strange it is a very unique feature that he sees is an island that is 8-miles wide, by over one hundred miles in length, as he flies over this island to the other side he believes he is returning back to the ocean on the other side, but this is not the case what his high resolution radar as detected is a sub ocean that is only five to ten feet in depth going from a couple hundred miles in length to a couple hundred miles in width this is quite incredible in flying over this narrow sub ocean and as I said it is only five to ten feet in depth now, about five hours later.

'Meridien', now has finally reached the other side of this moon, and before he heads home he then notices and gazes on an incredible sight a spewing volcano that is sending almost frozen nitrogen, little carbon monoxide and trace amounts of water or frozen water vapor into the Triton four hundred mile dense thick atmospheric band and now blanketing over two hundred miles of this Cantaloupe hilly terrain like a highly picturesque slowly falling snow similar to Earth but falling much slower because of Tritons gravity being less than Earth's moon, and this why it's so slow in its falling reaching to the surface here on Triton.

And, then passing over this spewing volcano and falling snow at this high safe altitude then Daxor proceeds on to the other side of this moon about a couple hours later the spacecraft, 'Meridien', will soon reach, Cosmoport Pod base but before it reaches there it will turn in an east-west tour and then he stops, he will then see this moons horizon with mostly a land continent to the south and the ocean to the north and now opening up 'Meridien', thrusters at one quarter speed, Daxor then moves on to map and investigate there shoreline and ocean as well.

At Cosmoport no. 6 mining Pod, Franz Waldheim, Jennifer Aldridge, Ramon Sanchez, and Anna Magdalena all now lowering the specialized truly built submarine with a specialized miniature thorium powered submersible with full onboard electronics and with a loaded miniature four torpedo launch tubes with a special electromagnetic rocket bullets and its ability to stay underwater for several Triton days and designed in staying there at a depth of six hundred feet. And, now going down the five foot wide narrow vertical hole is carefully land on the bottom ice floor below, then Franz Waldheim, Jennifer Aldridge, and Ramon Sanchez went down in their electric motorized repel harness backpacks and once down in the subterranean world they carried it to the seven hundred foot wide oval round pond and then gently put it into the cold almost frozen water and once into the water through its artificial intelligence software and specialized tracking interface by our orbiting spacecraft , Venture', with its deep penetrating radar that will track the submarines small thorium reactor in the submersible and will follow it to perhaps where the alien spacecraft was at its past coordinance frozen ice stay on the Triton surface.

Then the three scientists watching the submarine go down into the three hundred foot estimated vertical vent they went to the vertical hole and with their electric motorized backpacks they repelled back up one hundred feet to no. 6 mining pods, and once there roughly forty Earth time minutes, and when they came above and met Anna Magdalena at the control computer terminal console monitoring between Venture, and Cosmoport no. 6 pod and then Franz Waldheim took over the monitoring of the submarine going not only down the vent but now going up the river just underneath five feet and moving at five knotts towards where the alien spacecraft once were before it exploded.

As the submarine was going further in this river the vehicle was then incounting an underground cave and then it was now completely in an underwater cavern tunnel that grew larger expanding sixty feet in a near diameter and later into a pear shaped underwater cave going half way now further into the former alien site. While 'Venture Was tracking the underground submarine, out in space near Pluto 'mayday' signal is getting stronger and coming from somewhere on the equator of this sub-planet. And, Anna Magdalena now tracking the second freighter and Anna renaming it 'Nomad', and now with 'Nomad', at less than ten million miles from this sub-planet Anna put into motion with its dish antenna receiving commands from Cosmoport to slow down and prepare to orbit this sub-planet and allowing its artificial network system to secure a soft way to circle and orbit this sub-planet after it slows down and is grasped into its light gravity.

On the 'Meridien', Daxor cyborg robot, is now flying over and along the northern ocean and southern landmass coastline and the spaceship port side is photographing mile after mile of reverse upside down stagletites that are very sharp going up its spine needles in reaching heights of over two hundred feet, and going mile after mile ending at the shoreline of this southern coastline border and then reaching and slightly passing the landmass by turning port left into a northern ocean bay, he then turns his spaceship straight north towards a small frozen coastal land mass cape point and flying over it is now going into the ocean and now leaving the shoreline landmass completely behind the 'Meridien', now according to my radar has just come across an incredible sight in front of my spaceship on the moon's surface is an incredible ocean iceberg that is one hundred feet high almost sitting over an extreme frozen surface water line and with its two thousand miles in a triangular size shape with a submerged subwater depth of over two hundred feet down almost floating near its ocean bottom floor, what is so incredible is that this exist in this extreme cold of Triton almost four hundred minus fahrenheit degrees moon.

TRINEP 5-2, spacetime

The submarine is now in a small ravine chasm in this tunnel world going northeast towards the former alien site and then without notice two of these creatures came and attacked the submersible left and right hitting the submarine but with the submarines artificial intelligence defense software it avoided further attacks and then the submersible launched two of its rocket torpedoes hitting and entering the one creature and then killing the creature in it turning it petrified black completely dead with the other creature escaping and swimming fast to the northeast. The submarine then is now in a ravine that is becoming extremely hot around one hundred and ten degrees, and this creature seemed to survive in this hot world, said Anna Magdalena who is monitoring the submarine from the 'Venture', orbiting spacecraft which has a powerful three dimensional deep x-ray penetrating radar looking deep into this undersea tunnel ravine world. Now Franz Waldheim saying to Anna Magdalena that where did the one creature go and she said I do not know but it has disappeared.

Then the submarine encountered three smaller submersibles floating freely in this undersea subterranean world and the AI submarine looking into the broken glass window of one of the three submersibles were two of the aliens inside the flooded submersible were completely decomposed dead with their strange bone like features being revealed that these undersea creatures simply consumed these aliens for their food. Then the submarine moving forward went into a cavity of the continuing ravine world and found twenty of these sea creatures of various ages swimming around with this lone adult creature protecting them but the submarine was not stopping and simply moving on and the adult creature realized it was not going to invade their space and simply left it alone and the submarine went further on to where eventually it went and stopped under the five foot diameter hole that was dug by the aliens in there spacecraft that was once there.

While the submarine was stabilizing just under the vertical hole, high above the surface hole came the capsule shuttle pod no.1 hovering on top of the surface hole rim and lowering a special magnetic grappling hook pad and once down the hole attaches to the submarine and then carefully picks up the submarine and sends it through the five feet hole delivering above the surface and then the shuttle stabilized hovering twenty feet above the vertical hole rim and then a special cold weather canvass hood came over and under the hanging submarine and enclosed it in a warm thermal jacket and then the capsule shuttle pod took off and went back to the 'Cosmoport', settlement base.

Once at the SHOP no.6 Pod, they Franz Waldheim, Paul Stewart, Peter Walker, and Jennifer Aldridge took the submarine and disassembly it into its parts with artificial intelligence, with thorium reactor battery and the photo memory unit. Later that day they watched on the wall screen displays what the submarine saw down under in the subsurface ravine mini-canyon where the creatures seem to make their way into a warm water that is vented down below. With, Franz Waldheim stating that as long as they are there they pose a very real threat to this settlement base, they all agreed and I ask Ramon Sanchez to construct a vertical hole covering that will prevent these creatures from coming up the vertical hole to here in this no. 6 Pod.

Meanwhile, at the Shop no. 5 communications unit Anna Magdalena and coming into the no. 6 unit, Paul Stewart and Jackson Banes are now at their computer communications and looking in their deep space telescope and with their deep space robotic controlled computer console are now directing their newly renamed freighter to 'Nomad"spaceship into a sub-planet sub-orbit with the spaceship retro-rocket thruster engines in now slowing down the spacecraft so it can now put it fully into a one hundred thousand feet stationing orbit near or on top of the 'Mayday', signal. Now slowing down and after a third orbit it finally came to a stop at due altitude straight up north from its signal origin.

Now it is listening on a very strong signal, with clear reception and it switches from a 'Mayday' signal to an actual voice communication, and the two of them, Anna Magdalena and Paul Stewart with Jackson Banes, then immediately contacted the rest of the crew and Franz Waldheim to no. 5 communications and with all of them coming in the alien creatures trying to communicate with Cosmoport, and then Anna Magdalena said we may communicate them with pictures and then Anna sent some pictures to these creatures and they sent some of them to us and we started to transfer their language and we in turn sent our language to them.

They seemed quite friendly Franz Waldheim said to the other scientist. And they all agreed, then through our growing language database they wanted to know where are we and if they could come to meet with us and then Franz waldheim said to the other scientist I thought this was some kind of rescue, and Jackson Banes and Peter Walker said do not tell them where we are for this is becoming a trap for us, because if we tell them where our base is how do we know its one ship perhaps there are a couple of them that are in fine shape and not damaged and, Anna Magdalena fully agreed and then Franz Waldheim said to Anna Magdalena get the 'Nomad' out of its orbit and send it to 'Hippocamp', the smallest moon of Neptune and Anna Magdalena and Jackson Banes did just that and 'Nomad' left Pluto orbit headed for 'Hippocamp', and Jackson Banes said to the others it will bypass Triton and us in traveling three million miles distance outside of Cosmoport, base and then Anna Magdalena, said we will say a kindly goodbye to these aliens and be on our way immediately.

And sure enough not one Earth hour passed by, and the three alien saucer spacecraft followed 'Nomad' and then they attacking it parked the three alien spaceships on the hull of the 'Nomad', and then entered the spacecraft through the airlock hatch oval doorway, and then the scientist crew said to Franz Waldheim will you please initiate the self destruct code to the thorium reactors sub intelligence unit now or otherwise when they get to the bridge on board the 'Nomad' they will know exactly where we are, please Franz Waldheim and then he said okay to them you are right and then he said to Paul Stewart to initiate the self destruct countdown computer command code and set it for one second and then, and then he sent the command code, in it saying 'Goodbye Charlie', and the message was sent with a special discreet code that they will not know what it means or about and it was just sent, and we will know in less than twenty one minutes with Jackson Bane watching with our telescope aimed towards 'Nomad' and Pluto hopefully we will see the self destruct explosion on our console viewing screens.

Twenty-one minutes later there was a powerful explosion and they could see an incredible blast from here at Cosmoport base on their wall viewing screen and then they communicated where the 'Nomad' was once there and nothing from the spacecraft now exist not even from the aliens spacecraft who did not answer with their communication in reaching us for assistance. Now coming in on viewing screen with their communications loudspeaker the 'Meridien', spacecraft piloted by Daxor confirming the explosion of the 'Nomad', and with his voice now coming in quite loud and clear and saying to the crew that I have extremely valuable information to share with you, in speaking to them and saying that I am now less than five hundred miles away from Cosmoport base and will arrive to Cosmoport in no more than one hour's time until then, until then I am maintaining radio and video silence until you see me again.

Daxor cyborg robot yesterday coming back and then showing the entire crew members his astounding trip around Triton, and all of them were in complete awe and amazement of how incredible this moon really is with Franz Waldheim thanking Daxor for volunteering to go it alone and to record this fantastic data and photographic findings of this moon and said to Daxor that Anna Magdalena today will send this find and data to Earth who will most properly send several more scientists here in the near future to fully explore this moon, Triton.

Daxor working with Peter Walker, Mary Walton and Laura Philmore are working on a genetic poison that would kill these creatures once they come back here in the deep subterranean pond and the vertical hole. In the meantime Ramon Sanchez and Paul Stewart are finishing their work putting on a manhole hatch door covering on the vertical hole that will automatically open and shut down below with an open and close switch that is now part of the computer console accessory in Pod no.6 mining unit, on the now modified console in the event we could not kill the creatures at least we will be protected by them.

Jackson banes in SHOP No. 5 communications unit that also houses all astronomical camera telescope remote control of the two deep space telescope high resolution unit of 100 megapixel camera AI imaging console and its specialized viewfinder for nighttime, standard, thermal and spectrometer real time photography, is looking at the former site of the 'Nomad', explosion and discovered something quite odd there is one small pod ship acting like a space buoy just floating there sending out a weak signal to Anna Magdalena and Daxor who was there they the magnified the communication signal with full dampers and filters on and Daxor said to Banes you are quite right, there is this signal and its a multi-photographic one and with Daxor mini supercomputer processor brain analyzed the pictures in a unique order and Daxor said that this creature needs our help e is the lone survivor of the three alien spaceships and he is in stasis cryogenic sleep until you reach me. Anna Magdalena now went to Franz Waldheim and told him of this find and said to me should we attempt to rescue him and she said yes for we can learn a lot from this alien being and he said yes, and she said to him I am taking Daxor and Paul Stewart with me and we are taking the Meridien spaceship and we are leaving in thirty minutes from now.

The no. 2 Pod shuttle capsule then took off and went to the 'Meridien', spaceship and once on board checked all systems to ensure the spacecraft can make the journey and Daxor said all systems are fine and ready for launch towards pluto. Then the spaceship 'Meridien', took off from its parking orbit and with all thrusters on it was sent to Pluto and to the former site of the exploded spaceship 'Nomad', and to the lone alien space buoy in cryogenics sleep waiting for us to come by and rescue it. While in transport to the alien space buoy, Anna Magdalena was speaking to Paul Stewart and Daxor in her saying to them just before we reach this alien about roughly about one hundred and fifty thousand miles from it, we will send the No. 2 Pod capsule shuttle with you Daxor as its pilot in it and when you reach the alien space bouy you will then attach the special magnetic interface wired cord plate on to the alien hull surface from your tether towing capsule Pod attachment unit and where you will then determine its atmospheric life support systems and then while coming here to 'Meridien', spaceship you will inspect and supervise its entire on board communication and or tracking systems if it has one and you will let us know if there is any possibility of a trap by them where one or two of the alien spacecrafts might have managed to escape and Daxor said yes to her, I will comply to your given instructions.

When 'Meridien', reached its destination at one hundred and fifty thousand miles from the alien space buoy Daxor went into Pod no.2 shuttle and reached its destination two hours later, finding the small space buoy was no problem and Daxor in Pod no. 2 shuttle just stood there keeping radio silence and then after thirty minutes he released the magnetic clamp tether clamp system and targeted the magnetic clamp to the space buoy and off it went with its small powerful thrusters hitting the hull of the space buoy and then Daxor immediately went to work setting up his and interfacing it with the aliens on board computer system, and any tracking device the space buoy is implementing or sending out and Daxor then after ten minutes of silence radioed back to the 'Meridien', spacecraft and Anna Magdalena and to Paul Stewart that everything seems to be okay with this silent space buoy with no hostile measures of any kind present.

And, now Daxor cyborg robot radioed back to the floating silent 'Meridien', spacecraft that the space buoy on board computer appears that the aliens cryogenics sleep systems seems to be okay and his entire stasis is quite normal for a pickup, and now I am with my tether extended set at maximum five hundred feet between us, we are now moving slowly and in dragging this space buoy to our fixed coordinates location and we will wait for you to pick us up once we get there.

On board the 'Meridien' spacecraft Anna Magdalena and Paul Stewart were discussing once we reach Daxor then we will notify Cosmoport to create a security fenced in area in the Shop pod No. 8 and we will monitor his condition and then we will start to truly communicate with this alien creature coming from somewhere in outer space maybe in another solar system that is near to us said the two of them with complete radio silence as they were headed to meet up with Daxor. Three hours later 'Meridien', has located the the shuttle capsule Pod, in the near distance with the tether rope cable towing the the alien life buoy behind it, and parking next to the space capsule pod Daxor cyborg put the pod into the spacecraft hanger hatch and then created space for the alien life buoy with Anna Magdalena and Paul Stewart and then they reeled in and hauled the space buoy into the new space hangar and then Anna Magdalena stayed with Daxor who was watching the vital life signs of the alien inside residing in cryogenic sleep, while Paul Stewart piloted the 'Meridien', spacecraft back towards Triton.

Paul Stewart said through the spaceships intercom to Daxor and Anna Magdalena, that there is no other alien spaceship at all within ten million miles of 'Meridian', and she then said back him and Daxor I believe this alien creature is the only and last one to escape the 'Nomad', explosion and what I am saying to you is we can now speed up and we should get there in less than two hours flight time. Daxor then said to Paul and Anna should I contact Cosmoport to arrange for our coming and to make sure we have a place to hold this alien in SHOP Pod no. 8 unit enclosure.

Four hours later the spacecraft 'Meridien', is now in Triton orbit and Anna and Paul took the alien and put the creature in the space capsule shuttle pod and one hour later it landed at the launch receiving pad and its pad mover at cosmport, putting it into the SHOP Pod No. 8 unit and meeting the rest of the crew who then transferred the alien into special holding enclosure unit for a complete medical evaluation. The recovery bed with full diagnostic analyzers monitoring with Peter Walker, Mary Walton, Laura Philmore and Daxor looking on and with their reserved medical supplies now being used to help recover the alien which is now off cryogenic stasis sleep and now according to the ECG multi heart beating AI setting unit what the group believes to be its normal dual heart beats.

Now simply waiting for it to recover in the enclosed holding pen that will be fully secured by Earth's penal standards, it will be 24 hours monitored and its dual heart beat constantly watched with an immediate alarm system if anything happens. In the meantime Daxor, Anna Magdalena and Paul Stewart were inspecting the alien life buoy escape craft for clues about these creatures, and analyzing how their on board computer works.

The fully restrained at its bed is the six foot tall alien creature looking similar to a reptilian with four fingers, one head slim body and feet similar to humans with scales on them and most of the body, Daxor is now washing the creature down and looking at its teeth with semi-sharp incisors and several lower molars not unlike humans. Then without warning except for the ECG machine then the alien creature woke up and Daxor called the entire crew to come to Shop No.8 unit and they did and the alien that is now startled was when the crew came made this alien at first frightened and then calmed it and after their initial reception the creature then calmed down and Anna Magdalena said to the creature gesturing with her hands coming to her mouth and rubbing her stomach, and then the creature looking at them in it shaking its head said yes and there was food on the rolling table at the side of the bed and the creature looking at it shaking its head said yes, in shaking its head in full agreement and they fed the alien with soup and solid food and it took it and smiling became rested and with its smile which is the universal language for everything is okay said Franz Waldheim looking on and then said to the alien creature with Franz Waldheim gesturing can you breathe this atmosphere, and looking at him said yes. Then they allowed the creature to rest with Anna and Daxor staying behind to care for the creature and then trying to speak to the creature with pictures and then they released the aliens forearm restraints, but not its feet restraints and they served more food, then they had several kinds of music and then they played it to the alien creature who was open and smiled listening to the music piece, while the others went on to their individual Shop Pod units satisfied that this alien creature for now means no harm to us.

TRINEP 1-3, spacetime

While working down into the subterranean underground terrain at the pond intake water nozzle hose Ramon Sanchez and Peter Walker, finishing in putting on a special underwater electric antenna monitoring sensor that will let the Triton crew know when and if these animal creatures would come up to the underground pond surface. When sure enough they put on the warning signals and it indicated that it is not a drill but there is now tremendous activity two hundred feet down below the seven hundred foot round oval pond. Then they immediately finished and ran to the vertical hole going up the tunnel hole and they then closed the hatch manhole covering and at the shop No.6 Pod unit they watched on the view screens the five creatures in coming up staying a full fifteen Earth minutes and coming close to the manhole covering for five minutes then the five left and went back into the pond and diving back down to where they come from. And, then the entire crew came in and watched the trail end of the excitement and Franz Walheim said ,we have to understand that these creatures mean us harm and we now have to arm ourselves and create heavier specialized armoury with these special bullets created by our team to kill these creatures once and for all.

What do you mean said Laura Philmore speaking to Franz Waldheim, what I mean is that in two Earth weeks we will send four submersible crafts that would be fully loaded with these specialized torpedos will kill everyone of these creatures we could find and that's an order and my instructions will be obeyed.

Meanwhile at Shop No.8 Pod unit Daxor and Anna Magdalena are taking very good care of the alien creature and have given it a name, they call it now 'Rohn', and its vocabulary has greatly improved to the point he understands enough simple english to ask for things and to help out with astronomical findings in telling us were 'Rohn', is from.

Now 'Rohn', is free from its restraints and able to walk about and seeing the technology of these humans and Franz Waldheim then meeting 'Rohn', in Shop No. 8 unit now speaking in a very simplified english which it understands and able to converse back to Franz Waldheim, and then Franz Waldheim said to everyone that 'Rohn', will be free to walk about our 'Cosmoport', settlement base here and I want everyone here to speak to him in a simplified english and if you would kindly upgrade his english knowledge and then speaking to Daxor, you for now will be responsible for its care, and Daxor complied and now speaking to

'Rohn', I will take care of you now, and it understood and complied back in english saying yes to Daxor back.

With 'Rohn', in Shop No. 5 unit, watching the computer screen and a review by Franz Waldheim and Anna Magdalena with Ramon sanchez, looking at the view screen, commenting about these water animal creatures, Franz Waldheim said to Ramon that we need a greater explosive yield with these rocket torpedo bullets to take down and kill these creatures, listening in looking at these alien creature on the viewing screen, 'Rohn', interrupted them and said there is an easier way to either kill these creatures or simply shrink them down to their normal size, now puzzled Franz Waldheim, Anna Magdalena and Ramon Sanchez turned around and looking at 'Rohn', and Franz Waldheim said what do you mean shrink those creatures?

The alien then said again, yes what I mean you can shrink these creatures to their normal size and you can use your rocket torpedo bullets to do it by injecting these creatures with a special antigen bacterium that will not take that very long for this antigen to take effect and the creatures will then gradually return back to their normal size. Then Franz Waldheim said back to the alien creature, what do you mean return them back to their normal size, and the alien, 'Rohn', said we have used these creatures for on board electrical backup if anything would go wrong with our power supply unit and these creatures when small do not have the power supply we could use so our scientist created a specialized growth antigen hormone that would increase their mass and size of these creatures. Can you give us or make this growth antigen formula to us and 'Rohn', said yes I can, and then Anna Magdalena took 'Rohn', to Shop Pod No. 4 chemical unit and that Anna Magdalena said to Peter Walker, Mary Walton and Laura Philmore, and Anna Magdalena said to them that 'Rohn', will develop a special antigen hormone that will shrink these creatures and from there finally destroy these thirteen foot dangerous creatures.

Then 'Rohn', came in to Shop Pod No. 4 unit with plans and samples of the rocket torpedos that you will conform to put the antigen in its nose delivery system, let me know what you think said, Ramon and then he left and several Earth hours later they contacted Ramon to come back to No. 4 unit and when he came they said to him we are now finished thanks to 'Rohn', helping us then Ramon carefully put the chemical vile into the injector projectile unit and then he put this carefully put it into the torpedo bullet missile and carefully allowed the needle to be placed where once launched the torpedo bullet missile will inject the antigen into the creature and releasing the antigen chemical sirum. Then Laura Philmore and Daxor got an ingenious idea and confirmed it with Daxor, where both of them saying that the new electric receiving antenna that was installed by Ramon, she and Daxor said why don't you send an electric charge through the antenna and in turn sending the electric charge deep inside the water and by doing this it may attract these creatures there to the pond surface. Then 'Rohn', said that would attract these creatures would surely come and that is also a way we had used this concept for our needs. Then everyone said that is a great idea and now everyone has gotten to work and several hours later there was enough inventory antigen rocket bullets while Anna Magdalena and Ramon created a way to send several multiple electric charges through the pond water to attract these creatures to the surface with the four armed submarines on the subsurface rim around the pond. Ready soon to launch these antigen rocket bullets.

TRINEP 2-3, spacetime

Today's breakfast at the mess hall in SHOP No. 2 unit in which our new member 'Rohn', is in his own way smiling and showing great interest as to what humans do in this daily ritual of 'Breakfast', and now he is trying for the first time the taste of coffee and it seems to please him and the crew headed by Franz Waldheim saying to 'Rohn', will for now you will be working in the biological greenhouse foods unit, would that be okay with you 'Rohn', and he said yes that is fine, and thank you, then we have this one spare uniform and spacesuit unit and we will have a special bedding for you and now you will be working with Arlene Cummings, and would that be fine with you Arliene and she said back to Franz Waldheim I will stay with him and teach him about our new greenhouse farming technology in providing Cosmoport base growing food supply, and 'Rohn', looking at Arlene smiled at her in thanking everyone for this opportunity working for everyone here. They all said you're welcome and then now some of will have to follow down below and set up and now be ready to take care of these creatures. And, then later they went down except for Mary Walton, Laura Philmore, Arlene Cummings and 'Rohn', they remained at the surface, and now inside the vertical hole one hundred feet to the subterranean underground world.

They set up shop up shop with their equipment and foursubs down below and now Paul Stewart and Ramon Sanchez are putting the four armed submersibles into position around the pond and the rest of the team put themselves into strategic positions on the surface around the pond and now waiting for the creatures to come to the surface and be completely taken care of with this new chemical antigen ready to fire and penetrate these creatures once and for all and with Franz Waldheim communicating with Ramon Sanchez who is close to the vertical hole and his remote control display unite for the submersibles and said to Franz Waldheim I am ready when you are and Franz Waldheim said to everyone are you ready and they all said yes we are and Franz waldheim said to Ramon Sanchez let us engage our enemy and go to Ramon, and he then he turned on the electrical voltage and they all waited patiently for fifteen minutes and then Ramon said to everyone they are coming, and then he said again all of them, the entire family of these creatures are now coming to the surface and one, two, three, four and so fourth came up to the pond surface and then underwater of the pond the submersibles launched their rocket torpedo bullets straight into the bodies of these creatures, while they then fired their rocket bullets straight into either their mouths or directly into their torso hearts.

These creatures at first stopped then they simply could not move in staying completely petrified then they all fell to the ground screaming and in the water they also were also petrified and floating on the surface like dead fish on Earth, and then something is happening and most of the crew seeing an incredible sight, they actually saw these creature began to shrink and getting smaller and Franz Waldheim saying to everyone that these fast shrinking creatures are now becoming so small that these creatures are now dying and their bodies are slowly turning black and those that were in the water are now sinking going down into the depths of the water, while on top those creatures also turning black is becoming small enough to handle by the crews glove holding a lifeless creature that once caused great terror to these 'Cosmoport', scientists.

Everyone now is coming back to the vertical hole bringing there equipment and the three submersibles with them, except the forth one in which Ramon is retrieving by nose diving the submersible down the pond water depth of two hundred feet and sucking up like a vacuum cleaner all eight of the once powerful creatures that are no bigger than three inches and putting these creatures in the container and he then remote controlled the submersible to the surface of the pond where he picked up the submersible from the ice surface, then carrying it to the vertical hold with a rope descending down to pick up the submersible into the vertical hold, and while waiting there was a warning indicator on the display tablet he was working down here getting stronger and the coming out of the pond was this one creature going and coming for Ramon Sanchez and Ramon in the last seconds took out his special rifle that is loaded with the antigen serum rocket bullet and pinpointed it in his open mouth and then stopping and barely fifteen feet from Ramon Sanchez and now falls down gradually becoming petrified and turning black and getting smaller reducing its size from thirteen feet to three inches in seven minutes, waiting until the antigen serum is finally completed he then put the once creature into his satchel, and then he put on his specialized rappelling harness rope to his suit and he then motorized up to the surface and joining the rest of the crew in the mess hall in SHOP No. 2 unit.

TRINEP 3-3, spacetime

At the mess hall the crew talked about expanding Cosmoport and Franz Waldheim said to them any ideas or needs that your SHOP Pod units might want to grow or expand, and 'Rohn', said to Franz Waldheim and the others present at their breakfast meeting, and said I would like to enlarge the greenhouse with your expansion pod, and Franz Waldheim could not disagree and he said to the others are there any objections and no one disagreed with 'Rohn', and then Franz Waldheim agreed with 'Rohn', and said we will begin later today and start the expansion of the greenhouse. Franz Waldheim said to Daxor can you work with 'Rohn',and Daxor said it would be my pleasure. The job took two Earth days with 'Rohn', Daxor and their small construction crew of robot assembly sticks and their mobile track hauling vehicles, and when it was finished four Earth days later 'Rohn', spoke to Franz Waldiem and said to him can I put my cott in here with the garden and he said if you want to and he said thank you, now 'Rohn', and Daxor put the finishing touches placing tables, stools and chairs, lab equipment and containers for the garden and water distribution pipes and hoses to those containers that will carry the enlarged garden and then installing two water sinks one open and one closed and last 'Rohn's', cott to sleep on. Now finished they also expanded the toilet restroom and the shower cleaning room in the SHOP No.1 Pod unit.

TRINEP 5-3, spacetime

The morning breakfast and 'Rohn', said to the crew that I am working on a special liquid you might like, and Franz Waldheim said to "Rohn', your english and knowledge about everything here at Cosmoport is quite incredible and we thank you for being a good team member here and the rest of the crew said we truly thank you for your assistance as one of the team.Then 'Rohn',said I am working on a special food supply using your mushrooms and creating this fungi to have a various taste either like your fish or cow meat with a natural flavoring and taste that is quite natural and tomorrow I will present it to you and see if you would like it. They all said thank you to 'Rohn', Then Franz Waldheim said to Paul Stewart and Peter Walker you will be coming with me tomorrow and they said back to him where are we going and Franz said we are going to the western cantaloupe mountain hill ravine at five hundred miles from here that Venture, discovered yesterday in finding this ten foot wide vertical cave hole that is emitting thermal underground heat, and we will go with our No.1 capsule shuttle pod and find out what's below there, we will need three motorizing backpacks, extra thermal suit battery packs and ice pickers, and we are going to spend most of the day there before returning back here so when we leave tomorrow make sure you have eaten enough food to last you most of the day.

TRINEP 6-3, spacetime

The next Earth like day on Triton, they finished their extended breakfast and were leaving to go to Pod No.8 garage and a radio message came to Pod No. 5 communications unit Cosmoport base intercom, that in six days you will receive a new supply Freighter for your additional needs for the next two years, so enjoy what we send you, for it will have to last your scientific crew until we can send you any new additional supplies in two years time. Then after listening on the intercom they boarded capsule shuttle pod no. 1 vehicle and ten minutes later they were off for the western western cantaloupe mountain hill ravine. Landing next to the ice vertical cave hole, and now in the shuttle pod they got ready their equipment they will need and the three of them opened the hatch door stepped out in almost complete darkness with little ambient light except for the stars shining on them, and with their high beam 2-million lumens flashlights on they secured their backpack harness units to the shuttle pod and then one by one beginning with Franz Waldheim, Paul Stewart, and then Peter Walker, in their motorized backpacks they repelled down almost two hundred feet until they landed on a terrace flooring shelf looking at the scenery with their high beam flashlights there was an incredible range of colors like that of a rainbow on Earth.

Then they attached their harness backpack rope-cords to the vertical cave wall and then they noticed a kind of steps on the wall leading down ten stories and now the last landing steps they noticed this underground world light up like in a cathedral on Earth, the lighting is coming from these completely round ball crystals emitting this purest white lights and Peter Walker touching one of the crystal round balls felt heat coming from it and with their arm computer terminals they measured these crystal ball emitting one hundred lumens. The three of them completely in awe and surprised by these findings where they saw thousands of these round crystal balls light up everything down here they call a cathedral. Paul Stewart tried to pick up two of the crystal balls and found out he could not there was a mild electric shock he felt and his arm computer terminal briefly went out before its backup system came on so he then put back the crystal balls where he found it.

Franz Waldheim and Peter Walker looking at this were completely mystified and then Paul Stewart surmised maybe this is a life form community that does not want to be separated and for now they all agreed, then they went further in this small underground world, and then they came across a very hot seaming water hole that measures almost twenty-five feet in diameter their arm computer meares it to be one hundred and sixty-five degrees and looking on further there were several of these hot water holes around here. They went further into this small world and then they came upon a horizontal cave fifteen feet in height by ten feet wide and shining their high beams into this cave it goes well into the distance, where the high beam has a maximum lumens distance of one thousand feet.

Then Franz Waldheim decides to go into the cave and checking his oxygen and power suit energy levels which were good for him and

Paul and Peter checking theirs too, and then they entered the cave only going one thousand feet and if nothing happens we will then return back here and next time we will go further than one thousand feet and now moving into the cave they traveled not one hundred feet and these ceilings, walls and rock and the ground they are walking on has these shiny sparkling gemstones inverted with granite type rock, and Franz and Peter took their high beams aimed at the shiny crystal like rocks and they both said these are diamonds and Peter took and chiseled a few of these crystal diamonds and put them into his satchel bag to take back to Cosmoport base and to analyze them completely.

When they were finished they walked further on and heard from their helmet microphones that picked up a sound in the near distance further along inside this cave and when they came out the cave on the other side or back entrance and stood on a terrace like balcony they put their three high beams straight ahead and there was this immense underground waterfall almost as large as Americas, New York Niagara falls, they came out half way on this terrace now feeling the falling frozen cold water and shined it two hundred feet above them and two hundred feet down below and the falls ended below on a surface river that was seven hundred feet wide.

The waterfall was maybe eight hundred feet in width and they could hear the sound through their thermal Triton space suit helmets. As usual when ever they go on a Triton sojourn travel assignments they always take their day/night high resolution cameras and they took outstanding pictures and videos to take back to Cosmoport base. They stayed for no more than ten minutes and then they have to go because their oxygen and power battery units were less than half full and Franz Waldheim said to the scientist let us go and they then left to go back to the vertical cave hole and then reaching their they motorized (repelled) back up to the surface and to the capsule shuttle pod where later in the shuttle pod they were talking about this underground world where they took several pictures and taking these souvenir diamond looking crystals and then they took off for their Cosmoport base.

Three hour later at Cosmoport base in SHOP Pod No.3 geological unit, Franz Waldheim analyzed and tested the diamond looking crystals and told Paul and Peter, that I put these crystals through every test and my scientific analysis is these are diamonds and now you can rejoice and tell everyone we have a diamond mine on Triton. And, later that day at the mess hall Franz Waldheim told everyone about their find and Franz passed around the diamond and said to them I am also as you know a mineralogist and I know how to cut diamonds perfectly in any fashion cut you may like and in two days we are going back down there and I will bring a few crystalline diamonds with me. "Rohn', said to all that this stone to you are valuable and Franz Waldheim said yes, they are to 'Rohn', and the others present, and 'Rohn', said when I was on one of the saucer spaceships, in finding a place to rest and hopefully to find some food we landed on this huge world in the outer reaches of what you call the 'Kuiper Belt',with a thin atmosphere and with strange animals and plants and one of these animals was the creature you fought with in the subterranean world below, and then Jackson Banes interrupted the conversation and spoke to 'Rohn', and said too him what world are you talking about and he said later I will show you on the new map that you created here on Triton, and I will give you the astronomical coordinance where you can find it.

In the meantime everybody here I want to show you something I created and I hope you would like it, and then "Rohn', brought out his latest invention or distilling and he showed everyone in this karraff his creation and told everyone if you don't like it I will never produce (distillation) it again and bring out paper cups he poured it to the crew members and Franz Waldheim said to everyone you better sip it slowly this may give a kick and a high and sure enough they slowly drank it and they all said wow, oh my said the women and they for a brief moment said thank you. And Franz Waldheim said to 'Rohn', what proof is this and he said I believe one-hundred proof, he said back to Franz Waldheim.

Franz Waldheim said to 'Rohn', how did you make it, he said, I took Besault and granite stone which we have here and I then grinded it to a fine almost powdery form and then I went to your horticulture stockroom closet and took out your specialized plant hormone growth soil mixture, I hope you would not mind me doing so, In looking at Arlene Cummings, and she saying back to him, no I do not mind to, 'Rohn', and then he said I mixed it up and then putting it in a large bucket I put these blackberry seeds in this large bucket and putting this hormone growth spray and then, I put this acoustic rhythm music on it and it simply it grew in a matter of hours where I carefully watered it and then when it reached its maximum growth, then it was ready to be harvested I plucked it from its vines and then carefully distilled this berry and this is the end result what I have done, I hope everybody here likes it, and looking at Daxor, he said not to worry I am sure they will give you a special software that mimics intoxication drunkenness with everyone here approving of what 'Rohn', had created.

Later that Earth day Arlene Cummings, Mary Walton and Daxor , were helping 'Rohn', complete his greenhouse extension by giving him the spare reserve electronics high resolution imaging microscope and also setting him up with a small chemistry lab, Motorized ten speed mixing bowl and a work table research analyzer computer terminal setup. 'Rohn', thanking them in helping him to truly create a wonderful scientific workshop for our food and nutrition research with this greenhouse extension.

On the other side of this base, Jackson Banes with help from Paul Stewart and Anna Magdalena in helping him complete a small extension of SHOP Pod No.5 into a small planetarium platform with added electronics display and computer network terminals that can control the dish array, the deep space dual telescopes and the Venture spacecraft on board network systems from additional leftover housing materials that was not being fully utilized after the completed greenhouse extension setup.

It is the next morning Earth time on Triton at the mess hall where the team is having an improved breakfast with pancakes from 'Rohn', who gave it with condensed (jam like) sweet blackberry sauce, and newly created and harvested coffee beans fully grounded and with soy bean milk from Arlene Cummings and Mary Walton in their greenhouse labs. While each team member is eating their breakfast, Franz Waldheim was showing the videos and pictures of Franz, Peter and Paul in their underground adventures a couple of days ago, with everyone truly amazed about this underground world here on Triton.

Today is going to be a boring day where Franz Waldheim Anna Magdalena, Paul Stewart and Daxor is help erect a forty foot radio antenna next to the new astronomy unit, we will need one drilling walking stick and the cocoon tractor that will help place the rod stick ten feet in the ground, we take only two hours to do it. Franz Walheim said to Daxor you control the walking stick, Anna Magdalena you will control the cocoon tractor along with Daxor who will sit next to you in the cabin and Paul and I will be outside supervising the placement of the antenna rod, and with it securing the rod with six wires leading to the ground and attaching the electronic cables to the new astronomy Pod unit.

They worked two hours into their final round in installing the radio antenna, then there was something in space that both Franz Waldheim and Paul Stewart saw and immediately told the team and Jackson Banes to photograph it, and they are all looking at this incredible sight of fifteen very large saucers fly by past Pluto with their main engines opened and leaving a white-blue flame trail behind them and on they went as they appear to be only one billion miles further along in the heliopause from Pluto leading and headed into the Kuiper belt.

Later that day when they were finished installing the radio antenna and rod into the ground they discussed it in the mess hall and the first one he asked with all present were,'Rohn', and franz asked him are these your aliens perhaps trying to find you or your comrades who are now dead. And, he said looking at an enlargement of these pictures these are not my alien beings and their saucers are not from my species, they have a different architecture design than my species, and with Franz Waldheim being quite comfortable with 'Rohns', answer he then said to all for now there will be no receiving or sending of communications from Triton to Earth, and we will now take this command instruction into effect. And, before they left their mess hall meeting, Jackson Banes interrupted all of them and said a couple of Earth days ago I discovered this world that is larger than the moon but smaller than mars and looking carefully at this video pictures the distance from Pluto to this world is the same when we see the aliens with their 15 saucer spacecraft travel and going by further into the Kuiper belt. Franz Waldheim said to Banes are you sure yes I am he said and what we know and do not know is what could be happening on this Kuiper belt world past Pluto and what does it mean for us and Earth. Everybody is startled and fearful as to what could happen if there are advanced alien creatures who could posses a threat to us in the near future and then to Earth and mankind.

Three hours later there was a message and Anna Magdalena picking up the signal contacted Franz Waldheim and said to him should I receive it and he said is it from Earth and she said no it's from a freighter trying to reach us, and he said sure you may only receive this one, and I will also speak to them or its captain. This is the freighter 'New Adventure', come in Cosmoport, please come in and Anna Magdalena said we receive you and what is your distance from Triton, and the captain said that in two Earth days we should be in your orbit, and then Franz Waldheim said as you know I am the administrator here what is your cargo and personnel or any passengers you may have on board, yes I understand your request and I am sending you a mansfest and personnel and passenger listing and you should receive it before we reach Triton in two Earth days.

Franz Waldheim has received a message from John Abbott the captain of the orbiting freighter 'New Adventure', that they are ready for us to receive them. Franz Speaking to Anna Magdalena tell them that we have received your cargo manifest and also your listings of your crew and passengers, and we are leaving in 30-minutes and we will come on board in your loading bay in less than one hour Earth time. When they came aboard the 'New Adventure', everything was polished and squeeky clean and the six crew was very helpful to Anna, Peter and myself Franz Waldheim.

Captain John Abbott came back to greet us and said we are not staying here we are going to mars after our guest here disembark,and then coming back to the loading bay were Joanne Collins, Jeffrey Watkins and Allison Biels with their suitcase and other amenities around them ready to come on board their capsule shuttle pod to go down to Cosmoport. And, they got into the shuttle with Paul Stewart as pilot of the shuttle pod and he took off descending into Tritons limited atmosphere. Franz Waldheim, Anna Magdalena stayed on board and counted the manifest merchandise to be off loaded and to be sent down, once the shuttle has landed in the garage the new crew guests disembarked and was meet by the entire crew and escorted to their sleeping quarters, and then then Paul Stewart went up to the 'New Adventure', and regrouped with Franz and Anna, and then they loaded the merchandise on to the shuttle pod and Paul went down seven times and off loaded it inside the garage except for the last one, which was a new housing pod and that would be joined to the Garage and this pod contains the latest thorium reactor batteries that will last them for twenty-one Earth years on Triton. And, when the work was done except for the thorium batteries which will be the last to bring down, then the captain offered Franz Waldheim two somewhat large advanced replicators that are yours, one for material parts and the other for biological and chemical reproduction needs and John Abbotts crew snugly fitted the two large boxes into the space shuttle.

The thorium reactor pod has a small cockpit cabin and Paul Stewart would land that down near the garage. Well everything that was sent to Triton has been removed and the is goodbye now we have to go back to the inner planets and to mars, Captain John Abbott said goodbye to Franz Waldheim, Anna Magdalena, and Paul Stewart, in giving them a small other box and it was filled with liquor and chocolates that they might like, he gave it to Paul and said to them perhaps you may share it with the others down below, again good bye and the captain went to his helm up front, and paul went to the thorium reactor pod small cockpit helm and Franz Waldheim and Anna Magdalena went to the shuttle pod and the three took off and left the 'New Adventure', and now descending down to the Triton surface Franz, Anna and Paul could see the freighter, New Adventure', take off full blast with their booster thrusters in sending The captain and his crew back to the inner planets and to mars as his final destination.

TRINEP 3-4, spacetime

The next (Earth) day at the morning breakfast in the expanded mess hall table setting Franz Waldheim now has invited the three scientists to be permanent team members here at Cosmoport base. He said their names again to the others, and they are, Joanne Collins (geologist), Jeffrey Watkins (Mechanical Engineering), and then Allison Biels cyborg specialist (robotics, Programining) to the table and please all sit down and halve some some nice crepe blackberry pancakes with artificial soy sausage and our homemade coffee. Please sit down everyone and how are you three and I believe you came from mars,and they said yes. I am so sorry we could not speak to you three yesterday for us we had to do a lot of work installing and off loading our requested equipment and now my self Franz Waldheim, Anna Magdalena and Paul Stewart say a hello to you and I am sure everyone here helped to get you settled in your sleeping quarters and work stations, Alison Biels said the Daxor and 'Rohm' your alien member here I believe is an Utalu species member, truly helped us to aquant what living and working here on Triton is all about and that this is loyal and fun group that can always count on each other for assistance of any kind and the other two concurred whole heartedly.

That is good to hear and what strikes us the most is your alien crew mate in how is it possible that he could exist and where is he from, and Franz Waldheim said in all good time he will speak to you about his world.

Now I know we are having this fine breakfast, but now we have to partner up and to redistribute our workload requirements with fifteen members of people, alien and cyborg personnel here, and their specialized work needed by each of you and where each one of you will be placed and for now I Will be setting your skill sets and expertise, and I hope everyone here is okay with that, and they all agreed to accept my decision of the division of the workforce here. In one hour here I will call each one of you to this mess hall and tell you where you will be working and be assigned to and now please take a break and restup, and I will be calling you later.

<u>Departments and Team Members</u>

Geology: *SHOP (3) (6)* Franz Waldheim and Joanne Collins

Robotics: *SHOP (5)* Allison Biels and Paul Stewart

Horticulture: *SHOP (7)* Arlene Cummings Peter Walker and Rohn

Biology: *SHOP (7)* Laura Philmore and Mary Walton

Medical: *SHOP (2)* Laura Philmore and Mary Walton

Nuclear: *SHOP (8)* Jeffrey Watkins and Jennifer Aldridge

Commune: *SHOP (5)* Anna Magdalena and Daxor Cyborg

Engineer:	*SHOP (8)* Ramon Sanchez
Astronomy:	*SHOP (9)* Jackson Banes and Rohn
Library:	*SHOP (1)* Rohn and Daxor

After seeing each team member and where they will be placed, each scientist agreed and were very pleased with their station and grouping and each member were pleased with the other member's knowledge where we can learn from each other while performing our daily work requirement.

TRINEP 4-4, spacetime

The next Earth day on Triton the team member staff were having their usual breakfast and Franz Waldheim said to them how did everybody does with their partners if you had one for three hours yesterday and everyone was pleased and then Jackson Banes asked Franz Waldheim and the team mates that late Earth time yesterday and early this morning my telescopes detected this world, moon or asteroid a little over one billion miles past Pluto and then to my grief and concern these very large saucers I believe landed on this object and some other saucers took off going further into the Kuiper belt, and then on to and entering the Oops Belt Zone.

Franz Waldheim is quite shocked about this information and he has decided to send this information to Earth and hopefully they will tell us if we should make contact with them where that is the only course we can do here with our long range radio antenna dishes, and in the meantime not to be distracted about this we will unload our packages and cargo and distribute them to each SHOP team member, for now and when we get a message from Earth you all will be notified of the result, and also for now everyone here please try not to think about this distant world or asteroid at all beyond Pluto.

Then Franz Waldheim said to 'Rohn', what should we do here on Triton and he said that we should not contact these aliens, Franz said why not, and Rohn said what they are doing on this world or asteroid is an act of war where sometimes to build up their firepower for an invasion like on your old aircraft carriers a hundred Earth years ago, before the invasion begins this is our version of an aircraft carrier assault, and this is quite simply clear on their intentions in this solar system to go to war with your prime world, Earth.

They Franz Waldheim, Paul Stewart and Ramon Sanchez, took their two large cargo containers and then they completed their new deep space antenna and with its new high resolution spectrograph camera telescope with its infrared spectrometer equipment next to the SHOP No. 9 with this antenna and telescope we will now be looking at the dark world and will be used for only this specifically to learn whatever information we can know about with that dark world or asteroid in the Kuiper belt. They also got parts for their now four capsule shuttle pods to keep them going, and they completed the installation of the new thorium reactor batteries and keeping them off-line for now until we are ready to use them.

That evening at dinner (a scrambled morse coded) word came from Earth , and it said we made a short message, for you to send these aliens into the Kuiper belt stating that we want to somehow to contact with you, and the message then says **'Cosmoport_ Hello out there'**, keep on sending this message until they accept it or not for one Earth week, this message should reach them less than one Earth day.

TRINEP 5-4, spacetime

he next morning at breakfast time, Franz Waldheim spoke to the new established team members, and saying to them that I have a new message I received late yesterday Earth time. That this news from Earth, message said:

'you will take everything from your freighter 'Meridien' spacecraft that you can use for your needs down on Triton. When you have accomplished that you will then send that freighter past Pluto and then to send it to the dark world or asteroid', and then from the freighter 'Meridien', you will contact that dark world and by doing that you will monitor the freighter 'Meridien', performance and communications to that dark world'.

Now having breakfast at 0700 am Earth time, Franz Waldheim would answer any questions or objections you may have me answers. And, one by one said, Allison Biels asking Franz Waldheim, should we not evacuate Triton and go back to Earth or Mars, Franz Waldheim said no we should stay here and if we can create the first contact with these alien creatures (with 'Rohn', as an alien aside), Franz Waldheim saying to each of them we are the front line of humanity and we have to let these alien creatures know that and if we can make peace and share technology they may introduce us to faster than light travel to the next solar system as one example to meet them, and that is why we have to stay here and introduce them to us and who we are, now looking at Rohn would you agree with this assessment of the situation and 'Rohn', said, yes you are quite correct.

After answering these questions and objections that were rectified now the team have been told to make room for several additional equipment and find space for them. And, now the two groups going to the former freighter, 'Meridien', are;

Capsule shuttle Pod. No.1 (Franz Waldheim and Paul Stewart),
Capsule shuttle Pod. No 2 (Anna Magdalena and Ramon Sanchez).

The two teams will lift off from the garage at 11:00 am this Earth time morning, and then reaching the former freighter, we will now cannibalize the entire 'Meridien', and I mean we will take everything including also the one of the two thorium reactor batteries. The spare on board infirmary medical scanning unit. The spare parts for the capsule shuttle pods. And then the entire flight control system and flight recorder and whatever else we could use down here at Cosmoport. After we complete this work assignment we will then launch the 'Meridien, spacecraft towards the dark world or asteroid.

Then before leaving Franz Waldheim in the garage said the only thing you leave behind will be the two communication dish's and the on board multifunction night scope camera for us to view these aliens on this world. And, then thirty minutes later they took off for the 'Meridien', the former freighter spacecraft seeing perhapes for it the last time and now cruising up into space the two shuttle groups look at the former freighter while they gradually one hour later land into and come on board the shuttle loading dock. They get off the shuttlecraft and go to their prescribed locations and to go to their listed work assignments, it is now four o'clock, and they have now finished fully loading what they could or need into their two shuttle crafts and now before they leave Anna Magdalena activated a special program command into the spacecraft navigation and steering systems that if everything is okay nothing will happen to the spacecraft but if the aliens do take over this 'Meridien', spacecraft a special command will be set to self destruct in a silent countdown that will insure the only Thorium reactors will explode in a ten kiloton inferno, and, now they leave taking off for the Cosmoport base down below.

Once landed at the SHOP No. 8 garage Pod, the entire crew members were there in helping Franz Waldheim and others to take what they needed off the shuttle and to process it into their groups , and after two hours work at SHOP No. 5 pod communications unit Franz Waldheim, Anna Magdalena, Paul Stewart, with Allison Biels, and Daxor, and even 'Rohn', were inside SHOP No. 5 Pod and all were now looking at their Pod wall view screens and computer console terminals with lead communications officer Anna Magdalena is now commanding with the 'Meridien', spacecraft that has now put on a diagnostic that all systems are a go, has now put on the thruster's of the spacecraft, and with Franz Waldheim looking and is the official Cosmoport Administrator giving the go head, and has said to Anna Magdalena to engage the spacecraft to move and proceeding a computer command to go then the four booster thruster engines came to a full roar moving the spacecraft and also initiating the navigation coordinance on board computer towards that dark world and Daxor cyborg saying in 32-Earth days it will pass by Pluto, and in fifty eight days it will reach that dark world or asteroid cruising at 60-thousand miles per hour just inside the Kuiper belt with the two onboard dish antennas aimed and fixed on to the Triton Cosmoport base dish antennas.

TRINEP 6-4, spacetime

Again this is Cosmoport morning Earth time, everyone now sitting at the oval table setting with new foods now being served with, Arlene Cummings, Peter Walker, Laura Philmore, Rohn and also Daxor came and worked together to create the new food categories on the table and the dishes to eat. At the table is an artificial incredible tasting egg, tofu bacon realistically made cherry tomatoes and freshly made artificial wheat or oat bread with a new artificial orange juice and with freshly made tea. With everyone enjoying this new breakfast meal and Franz Waldheim saying to each other and today you will remain in your team groups and I will go to Each SHOP Pod unit and see what we can improve in your work conditions and work loads here. Later that (Earth) day there was a meeting at the mess hall in SHOP No. 2 habitat unit and now speaking is Franz Waldheim, who gathered around the table, that I want to thank you for speaking to me about your work conditions. With your new infusion of the 'Meridien', component and spare parts inside your SHOP units.

Later that Earth day SHOP No. 6 Pod Paul Stewart and Ramon Sanchez were finally completing a two person elevator lift device from spare parts and assemblies from the 'Meridien', spacecraft, and with that we can now not use our rappelling harness backpacks any more, we have a very nice grated flooring and a round cylinder protecting the two person lift elevator with a control switch on the cylinder that reads surface, below, and open and close hatchet man cover swing door. And Walking in to No.6 Pod is Franz Waldheim looking and seeing the testing of this new elevator from the handiwork of Paul and Ramon in creating this elevator device that will take no more than ten seconds to go down and twelve seconds to come back up to the surface. The elevator only is taking 90% of the five foot wide vertical hole space and leaving just ten percent for piping, hose and electric wiring and cable to the underground subterranean world. We also have lights and cameras, down below and we then positioned them like a walking trail to the seven hundred foot oval pond. Paul and I, Ramon also are inspecting and fixing the Cosmoport structural Pod housings with every secured inspected with a 100 percent okay and with the Pod's now better insulated from the outside extreme temperature of just under minus four hundred degrees.

TRINEP 1-5, spacetime

The next morning at breakfast time. Jennifer Aldridge, Jeffrey Watkins with Ramon Sanchez are now perfecting their thorium electricity power system throughout the Cosmoport facility base. The reasoning is that our communication and deep space requirements that can be achieved without reducing our power needs elsewhere in each SHOP Pods. And,Then Allison Biels, Paul Stewart, Anna Magdalena and Daxor were in SHOP No. 5 and were working on to improve their performance and memory of Daxor with 'Rohn', suggesting that in my escape life buoy has a special unit in my satchel holder contains a special unit that boosts the processing speed and with my language of Utalu and I will assist you in converting it your english tongue with my reptilian language structured tongue and they said to 'Rohn', thank you for assisting us. Peter Walker, Mary Walton and Laura Philmore are finishing upgrading and installing there water filtering and purification, and with assistance from 'Rohn', human and alien thorough anatomical diagnostic equipment template 3D screen display, and with its medical incision operating tools and disease analyzer and last their brand new dental care unit that sooner or later.

TRINEP 2-5, spacetime

It is another fine breakfast Earth day here on Triton, and the team members enjoying their blueberry pancakes and tofu sausages, fresh tree orange juice and a choice of a new decaff coffee or the regular a brew. And, while they were eating, Franz Waldheim speaking looking at the video and pictures of Daxor travels in the 'Meridien', spacecraft around the moon of Triton, and said last night looking at this information I think we need to investigate particular sites that could be useful for our needs such as:

- A large island with a semi-active island volcano with a thermal underneath spewing either water ice or water nitrogen and other released gas covering the island surface
- five to ten feet ocean depth going from several hundred miles to several hundred miles triangular size shape,
- reverse upside stagerites that are very sharp going up its spine needles in reaching heights of over two hundred feet, and going mile after mile ending at the shoreline of this southern frozen ocean
- Then there is a triangular size iceberg with a subwater depth of over two hundred feet down, almost floating near its ocean bottom floor. What is so incredible is that this extreme cold exists in Triton almost four hundred minus Fahrenheit degrees.

Also, here is the fact that at the north and south poles,there are tremendous thick ice snow fields of water ice under methane carbon monoxide with several hundred foot layers with an extremely smooth surface terrain that may be quite fragile on its top surface if you should stand on it, where you may fall tens of feet down into hardened unescapable condensed ice.

TRINEP 3-5, spacetime

Another breakfast day, the team members sitting at their seats talking about their Shop accomplishments and what we have created independently and as a group. With this Cosmoport truly being a small village like scientific escapement, that now we are truly an oasis in the vast darkness of this moon of Neptune and even near distant Pluto. Franz Waldheim asking each one, do we have any volunteers, in which I need to for two Earth days to go on capsule shuttle pod No.1 to take night sky space pictures for our benefit and then send it to Earth. Everyone in a nice way objected except for Paul Stewart and 'Rohn', the alien. Then Franz Waldheim said to 'Rohn', this will be your first away mission in where you will assist Paul Stewart in Mapping not only this part of the solar system but also Neptune and its moons, in much finer detail than we have from mars and Earth ever before.

They agreed to go and Franz Waldheim said later today you will be going at exactly 2:30 pm Earth time and you will be going with a modified shuttle with a mobile dual telescope one that is an infrared spectrometer and two, that is a wide angle 20mm lens with a night scope attachment, that Jackson banes will be installing it for you this morning after breakfast and you two will be helping him do it on the capsule shuttle pod No.1, and then you will be spending two Earth days and all information and updates will be handled and supervised by Jackson Banes our chief astrophysicist that would monitor your mission carefully, said Franz Waldheim at the breakfast table. It is now 2:30 pm inside the capsule shuttle pd and they are ready to take off, and in SHOP N0.9 Astronomy unit, in acting as mission control they saw the shuttle pod on the launch platform and Jackson Banes said to them are you ready and they said yes you will not engage your take off now, and then the two shuttle craft pilots took off rising at 100 feet per second and in one hour and fifteen minutes and went to a gravitational Apogee orbit of five hundred thousand feet.

The space capsule shuttle pod now half an hour into its orbit is slowly approaching the Triton north pole, and the two of them looking down on the surface of the moon north pole and see an extreme flat surface with this almost in the middle of this several hundred square mile deep snow plain a small semi-mountain ridge that is in their estimate to be over two thousand feet. And, then Paul Stewart looking into his viewfinder telescope camera, as the shuttle was passing around the north pole he saw past pluto towards the dark world or asteroid three huge spheroid shaped spacecrafts, that he believes to be one hundred Earth sized aircraft large carriers.

He showed it not only to 'Rohn', and Jackson Banes but also Franz Waldheim. Then the shuttle pod went around the orbit of Triton's north pole and now looking directly straight ahead is this large Neptune world and looking at its incredible size with almost a defused multi-stream blue-colored multi-stream airflow moving atmospheres in containing each of its layers of liquid hydrogen, helium, methane and our chemical analyzer in confirming it to be completely unbreathable. But what astounds Paul and 'Rohn', are the five rings in how extremely diamond-like and extremely shiny and so reflective almost like with Saturn's are; **Galle, Le Verrier, Lassell, Arago**, and **Adams**.are incredible but could be used for future mining opportunity.

TRINEP 4-5, spacetime

Franz Waldheim then speaking at the morning breakfast table with the entire team members is asking each of them we have to contact Earth and send them this alien information and video files, and it's up to them to take action regarding this dark world and its three huge saucers.

And, the shuttle came to a point of its orbit revolution of Triton where eight of its biggest of its other secondary moons become into their view:

- **Nereid**, all possible mining opportunities
- **Naiad**, all possible mining opportunities
- **Thalassa**, all possible mining opportunities
- **Despina**, all possible mining opportunities
- **Larissa,** all possible mining opportunities
- **Proteus**, all possible mining opportunities
- And **galatea**, all possible mining opportunities

and are now in perfect viewing and this is where Paul and 'Rohn', then slow down using their retro-thrusters of the orbiting shuttle craft and with their chemical advanced analyzer and camera system they recorded each moon in more detail, but only briefly and then went on to the next moon and now going towards the southern hemisphere they are now star gazing to our next door neighbor the alpha centauri solar system.

Meanwhile, life and work inside the Cosmoport is proceeding as usual with the expanding of this settlement base, and fixing any part of this base inside or outside that needs to be updated, and it is now 1:00 pm afternoon time at the mess hall with everybody listening and seeing on the mess hall view screen the two shuttle pod surveyors team members and with now everybody in total amazement, that they are five hundred thousand miles up orbiting the moon, while they have freshly newly made tafu stye schoen's and strawberry produced jam that is new to the table with fresh coffee or tea. Franz Waldheim has announced that Jackson Banes and myself will be in the astronomy SHOP pod No. 9 for the rest of the afternoon and with a sip from 'Rohns,' alcohol 90-proof produced homemade vodka.

The space capsule shuttle pod, several hours later has now come in for a landing at and then inside the SHOP pod No. 6 garage unit and is now parking the shuttle pod in its holding bay, and is met by Franz Waldheim and Jackson Banes who is congratulating them with their warm handshakes. They then went to the SHOP Pod No. 9 Astronomy unit where they were debriefed of their surveyor mission. Now in the Shop Pod No. 5 they were talking in finer detail what they saw as they were orbiting Triton.

Later that day just after 5:00 pm dinner time at the mess hall Franz Waldheim said to everybody present that I just sent the data and information file to Earth that Jackson Banes and 'Rohn', gave me earlier today and just a couple of minutes ago I got confirmation that they have received what I sent them. I am now asking everyone of you seeing what now lies beyond Pluto to that dark planet if you feel you want to go back to Earth I would understand and Paul, said no, Arlene, said no, Jennifer, said no, Ramon, said no, Peter, said no, Mary, said,no, Anna, said no, Daxor, said no, Laura,said no, Jackson,said no, Joanne said no, Jeffrey said no, Allison said no, and Rohn said no. and I Franz Waldheim say no too. It is now unanimous we will stay here in our full requirements of our contract for ten years stay until our replacement arrives, including you 'Rohn', with 'Rohn', nodding in full agreement and Franz Waldheim saying you may come with us stay here or greet and serve our new replacements.

TRINEP 6-5, spacetime

In SHOP No. 7 Greenhouse and its extensions are.Laura Philmore, Mary Walton, Arlene Cummings, Peter Walker and 'Rohn', are now very busy experimenting and expanding our food production with the last freighter sent to Triton. These genetically modified Caterpillars and snail (slugs) that were in cryogenic stasis sleep package mode are now alive and perfectly well that we will breed like in a miniature cattle farm in our special sectioned greenhouse that are enriched with protein and other nutrients that will be our mainstay meat food supply that we will have at dinner time as having a proper diet of meat, vegetables and fruit. Also from the freighter are; *grape tomatoes, avocado seeds, miniature carrots seeds, miniature cucumbers,vanilla plant seeds, red grape seeds,*additional *soybeans seeds* and stevia plant seeds and mushroom cultivation with other fruits and vegetables. Also from the last freighter were various plant supplies and nutrients, and specialized soils and ten pounds of sea salt with iodine and ten pounds of black pepper.

Next the garden greenhouse group were providing pipes, hoses and plastic covering tarps for their individual garden projects and caterpillar and snail farms. Afterwards controlling temperatures and specialized acoustic and sonic filtered sounds and music for each farm all coming from the 'New Adventure, Freighter'.

Anna Magdalena coming inside the Shop No. 9 Pod unit and meeting with Jackson Banes and Franz Waldheim in regard to the 'Meridien', spacecraft and she said the spacecraft tomorrow Earth time will be passing 'Pluto', I increased its top speed to 100,000 mph, and will now pass on by the dwarf planet 'Pluto', tomorrow morning and in three days it will pass by the moon 'Charon', and then in less than a week will reach the dark world or asteroid. Franz Waldheim and Jackson Banes said to her well done.

Also this morning I Anna Magdalena and Ramon Sanchez have installed the specialized solar panels to the SHOP No.9 Astronomy unit so not only to show how much we are truly collecting from the solar wind fields on Triton surface but also to measure and register solar (thermal) Ion radiation coming on to the surface of Triton, as well as to measure the electrical time in its conversion in analyzing the electrical field emissions being produced exhibited by the heliopause solar wind out here on Triton's surface by this new specialized solar installed panels, and it is now in place on Pod No. 9 and you can now analyze how much electrical and thermal solar radiation is now being felt in reaching us on Triton's surface by the sun at almost 2.8 billion miles away.

By the way Franz Walheim said hows the educational training by Daxor to 'Rohn', coming along, and she said pretty good 'Rohn', is extremely clever and is matching Daxor intellect by intellect in proficiency. For 'Rohn', has truly come a long way in being a true member of our team said, Anna Magdalena to Franz Waldheim, and then Jackson Banes interrupted by saying that I could need an assistant to help me with my astrophysics and other chores, can you assign him temporarily for a couple of days speaking to Franz Waldheim, Administrator here at Cosmoport base and he said to Jackson Banes yes I will and for now he is yours.

TRINEP 1-6, spacetime

It is now the next day on Triton, and now at the breakfast table the team members are sitting around talking. Franz Waldheim speaking to 'Rohn', and Jackson Banes said how did it go yesterday they both said wonderful, Banes said he truly knows his astronomy, very good said Franz Waldheim and now I am assigning two scientist-astronauts to go up for two days on the 'Venture', spacecraft and take the spacecraft to explore the rings of Neptune and do an orbital analysis of these rings in looking for any mining opportunities while we are here on Triton. The trip will not take long it is less than two hundred thousand miles away from Triton. Later that morning going into the afternoon Earth time, Rohn and Paul Stewart volunteered to fly the 'Venture', spacecraft to the rings of Neptune and Franz Waldheim said thank you to them.

And, they were almost about to go it when it started to snow here at Cosmoport from a nearby now very active volcano spewing nitrogen hot turned frozen liquid gas up into the thin atmosphere about one one hundred thousand feet according to the venture spacecraft flying overhead in orbit, and under space command directive rules the two travelers (Paul and Rohn) will have to wait until the snow ends or fly another Earth day.

With everybody now looking out of their oval portholes and or their main larger oval windows at Cosmoport, were completely enthralled, surprised and somewhat very happy this was happening to the team members now and all of them remembering years ago on Earth in seeing falling snow around their each christmas time or shortly thereafter now seeing it here on Triton. All of them also seeing this falling snow come down very slowly seem kind of magical and now with Triton's winds coming up now moving the snow at times horizontally, everyone here is astounded and the plans to see the neptunian rings will have to wait another Earth day on this moon. In the meantime while we mostly have nitrogen snow falling, a few of the scientists have gotten the idea to trap and capture it in their plastic buckets from the garage to filer and process it for our multiple greenhouses.

TRINEP 2-6, spacetime

The next Earth morning on Triton well after the last snow storm had fell, Franz Waldheim asked Rohn and Paul Stewart to come to his small office in SHOP Pod. 1 and asked them to bring a special communications equipment and camera telescope and set it on the Neptunian Moon, 'Nereid', you will still be going to the neptunian rings but not right now or tomorrow. He asked them would you volunteer or do you want me to select another two people, and 'Rohn', and Paul said we would be happy to go, when do we leave, Franz Waldheim said right after breakfast in two hours, oh by the way this moon is no more than one away from Triton and you will be there for at least two Earth days by the third Earth day you will have the equipment running and then you must leave, and they then said why must we leave, because you will be very near Pluto and beyond that the dark world or asteroid and I don't want these aliens to know of our existence quite yet. But while you are there please take out three hours, if possible and you will take this high powered thermal infrared night vision binocular telescope that you will take from the garage inventory, I will speak to Ramon Sanchez who is our inventory keeper and say it's okay to do so. Three Earth hours later they are in the SHOP No. 8 garage unit and Ramon is giving the the equipment they would need, and now fully loaded into their space shuttle pod they then take off a few minutes later to the orbiting 'Venture', spacecraft.

Once in space they dock at the loading spaceship dock, then they check all systems and it seems okay to go and then they initiate burn and they then put on their main rocket boost thrusters and they are off to see and plant a communication and solar system camera surveyor and telescope setup and away they went with a powerful roar after burn boost of twenty thousand thrust pounds per second thrust rocket engines moving the spacecraft headed to Nereid. They spent most of the Earth day looking out at this part of the solar system and then they see the 'Meridien', spacecraft with their long range viewscope moving half way past Pluto and coming near Charon its sister dwarf planet or moon. It will then be another day before they come across Nereid third largest moon, and the most distant moon of Neptune.

TRINEP 3-6, spacetime

The 'Venture', spacecraft is now approaching the moon Nereid and it is an irregular kind of oval shaped body that is similar to Earth's moon with no atmosphere being totally exposed to its space environment elements with a dark gray soot surface with the usual craters and several large what you might call exposed hills on it. Now the 'Venture', spacecraft has chosen an orbit close enough to one of those exposed hills that have an excellent view of the solar system where Paul Stewart and 'Rohn' are talking to each other and they have agreed to located their communication and space camera equipment on that one particular exposed hill on Nereid. They put their 'Venture Spacecraft on robotic mode and then they took their capsule shuttle space pod down to that exposed hill which has a small like terrace to land on. Once landed they immediately made sure that the rocky surface was strong enough and the surface rigid enough to support their equipment and then they took out from the space shuttle and started to erect their communication and space telescope and camera equipment and it took them several hours to install this doing it.

And, now they connected their small unused 'Meridien', 28 year life warranty thorium reactor battery and made sure its connections was strong enough to last and then when completed they contacted Cosmoport, and getting a strong confirmation signal in receiving their transmission from the two array dish antennas and also they installed a twenty five foot high secured radio antenna pole along with their dual multifunction telescope and camera.

They then did some diagnostic system programs checks to make sure it is working from their space shuttle and before they left they took and collected some moon soil samples in a couple of locations and picked axed a few surface rocks and put it in their holding containers, and with their personal cameras on their spacesuits, and then they took some snapshots of themselves and several snapshots of Triton and Pluto and the dark world or asteroid, and when they were finished They then took off for the 'Venture', spacecraft and space docked in their loading bay and several minutes later they took off to come back to their new comfortable home at Cosmoport base, on Triton.

Coming home the next day. They gave Jackson Banes their cameras and he then downloaded and then Banes saw something quite odd what he saw was this dark world or asteroid leaving the solar system and entering the Kuiper belt in leaving and going back and said to himself I must tell Anna Magdalena and Franz Waldheim to immediately stop the 'Meridien', from passing Charon or they may see the spacecraft as a hostile act, he then contacted the two people and immediately they came into SHOP no. 9 astronomy unit and said what do you mean, what I mean is you must stop 'Meridien', from passing Charon or our goose is cooked they will look at this war. What I mean is the dark world or asteroid is moving out of this solar system and why don't we allow it to leave, and say goodbye to them.

Franz Waldheim then commanded Anna Magdalena to stop the 'Meridien', and return it back to Triton, she immediately ran to the SHOP No. 5 Communications Command robotic unit console and then sent command signals to 'Meridien', and just as the spacecraft was about to pass by the dwarf planet or moon with the retro rockets breaking the speed which came on as the main thrusters shut off, and it took almost one thousand miles further on before it finally stopped, and I believe according to Jackson Banes said I don't believe they saw the 'Meridien'. Spacecraft and now still floating in space next to the dwarf world of Pluto, and then assured he said there was no action at all taken by this dark world or asteroid. And, slowly Anna Magdalena through long range remote control has reversed the spacecraft and called it back towards Triton with Jackson Banes saying to everyone that it was a close call and now we can all relax with these aliens not realizing we were here spying on them and their activities.

Then Jackson Banes put on his remote console screen to the Nereid communications unit and multi camera system and the transmission signal was extremely strong then Jackson Banes put the camera telescope on and aimed it to the dark world or asteroid moving into the distance and at the Cosmoport Base, they all saw the aliens then go back into the Kuiper belt.

Later on after lunch there was a meeting with everyone in attendance and Franz Waldheim said what does everyone think about what just happened here with the alien dark world, and Jackson Banes said these aliens must have somehow come here by riding this dark world into our solar system by just stopping there at this dark world or asteroid and found it was now slowly leaving the Kuiper belt and with its elliptical orbit was just now entering our main solar system without our knowing about their presence, and being there found that this world provided their makeshift means to resupply and rebuild their saucer spaceship fleet and were simply waiting and eventually moving on to other worlds or even solar systems by this dark world or asteroid to eventually swing around and go back inside towards the Kuiper belt. Then Franz Waldheim said to everyone, do you concur what Jackson Banes just said and one by one thinking about it said, yes he may be very right in his assessment,

Anna Magdalena said to all present, having their cup of tea or coffee and homemade bread, soy butter and blackberry jam looking at the last videos of the dark world or asteroid going back into the Kuiper belt. And, Then Anna Magdalena said to all the 'Meridien', spacecraft is moving at twenty thousand miles per hour and should be in orbit here next to the 'Venture', spacecraft at Triton in three days, with Franz Waldheim saying I really did not want to expense and give up a fine backup spacecraft that we may need in the future, and that they all agreed now getting up and going back to their individual SHOP Pod units.

The next breakfast day at 7:00 am the crew members spoke of our ability to expand our base and perhaps to look here or somewhere on Triton to create for the future a small mining and scientific community city of the future and now that we have 'Meridien', spacecraft back we are going to have to do a thorough topographic surface radar mapping with the help of Daxor initial data and photographic information. At 3:00 pm Earth time Anna Magdalena, Paul Stewart, Daxor and 'Rohn', blasted off from the Cosmoport launch pad base.

And, now a half an hour later they entered the spacecraft loading bay and taking out their equipment and installing it on the 'Meridien', and then the four of them took off the robotic navigation mode, and now they are going to spend two days fully mapping and radar image mapping Triton from space at an altitude of five hundred thousand feet.

Anna Magdalena is the Main Pilot
Paul Stewart is the Co-Pilot, Radar and photography
Daxor is Navigation
Rohn is Communication and flight systems

The 'Meridien', spacecraft is now according to Daxor will soon cross over into the Triton northern ocean, and Anna Magdalena said no this surveyor sojourn is to go over only the southern continental land mass and seeing the ocean she turned portside and went south and created a flight pattern to go over 48 % of the total moons continental land mass. Traveling in a particular circular hemispheric pattern Paul Stewart began to Radar image and Photographed the surface of this land mass. The process is a thorough one and a slow going one and that's why it will be at least one to two days work on this moon.

Several hours later they completed one quarter mapping and photographic imaging.and then they stopped the 'Meridien', spacecraft to have a lunch-dinner meal and to also to recharge Daxor internal batteries, now floating in near moon orbit they will take one to two hours rest, before they continue.their process and also in contacting Cosmoport of what they have already accomplished. After their lunch-dinner they were back at the spacecraft helm and then something incredible happened there was down below on one of the volcanoes they thought was dormant and incredible eruption of mostly nitrogen spewing out into the atmosphere of this moon in reaching almost as high as the 'Venture', spacecraft in near orbit. With Anna Magdalena at the pilot's helm, she just in time immediately put on her console vertical thrusters and then the spacecraft accelerated in going up to thirty thousand vertical feet and then slowing down they looked at this sight where this spewing volcano was producing an incredible amount of snow over one thousand square miles radius and blanking the area of with spectacular white nitrogen snow. Then after a few minutes later she then accelerated the thruster engines forward the 'Venture', spacecraft and then fifteen minutes later Paul began to radar image the ground again. And, after twenty minutes on the other side of Triton they came across an area down below to the surface and Paul said to Anna please stop and she did said to Paul in transferring the image to the helm control view screen they Anna, Paul, Daxor and Rohn, looked at the surface and then Rohn said to Paul what are we looking at and Paul said this very wide hole our sensors estimate to be two hundred feet wide on a fairly flat mountain hill plateau surface is perfect for our next and largest moon base that according to my calculations and AI computer topographical information is five to six stories down and with at its wall sides of six story entrance tunnels and I will record this information for a few minutes and then we can move on.

As they were completing their mission around the southern Triton hemisphere surface their sensors came across an interesting find in a small cantaloupe valley that was metallic and they decided to go down to the surface with their capsule shuttle craft, and a few minutes later they landed down onto the ice surface valley and went to the metal object, which was covered with strange language markings. Paul and

'Rohn', looking carefully at the metal and its markings found a loose alloy part with its markings and then they took photo pictures of other alloy metals and markings and went back to their capsule shuttle craft and blasted off to the 'Venture', spacecraft orbiting above. Once inside the spacecraft they put the alloy metal with its alien writing on it in the loading bay holding container. Now one hour later they came back over the Cosmoport base and then putting the spacecraft on robot remote control, they left on the capsule shuttle pod craft.

TRINEP 5-6, spacetime

It is breakfast time the next day at Cosmoport, and Arlene Cummings and Mary Walton are now serving a new breakfast item, and it is a new artificial salmon looking flesh piece with artificial tafu eggs with blueberry preserves over soy flavored whole wheat substitute toasted bread and served with vanilla latte coffee. Later that Earth day Franz Waldheim and Jackson Banes in speaking to 'Rohn', and said do you know anything about this alloy material and its writings on it, and 'Rohn', said back to them I do know about this material and writings that comes from the '**Orikata**, space bearing tribal race that are fierce and dangerous nomads in going from star system to star system looking for planets to colonize and create bases to perpetuate their lifestyle and technology system, and this material you are showing me looks and feels just like it in feeling quite new. And, then he said that your Daxor downloaded our database in our space rescue buoy and he must have also downloaded our space travels in the last three hundred years of our space travel technology.

Daxor and 'Rohn', speaking to each other, about the alloy metal fragments with the printed alien writings on it, and with Daxor then retrieving the database on the alien spacecraft storage information now has confirmed what 'Rohn', as just said to Franz Waldheim and to Jackson Banes about these beings, called the 'Orikata'. At Shop 1 pod unit, Daxor and Rohn were looking through the database that Daxor retrieved and created from his downloads from the exploded alien spacecraft and handing it over to Rohn to verify its meaning and in particular these alien writings on the metal fragments. The two of them spending three hours carefully in cross referencing their database with the pictures taken of the crash site scene are slowly piecing together a story of what all of this means regarding any possible contact in the future with us. Franz Waldheim and Anna Magdalena came into the library and looking at the evidence of photos, and folder information said there is something that we feel is simply not right with this information you are providing here to us and Franz Waldheim said what is that symbol on this alloy fragment and 'Rohn', said if you were to convert it into english it is a representative of a numeric '2215', and Daxor agreed. Then Franz Waldheim said that today Earth time it is April 3rd 2215, and both Daxor and Rohn were completely surprised and together said to Franz Waldheim and Anna Magdalena it now makes perfect sense that sometime this year as measured by Earth time these alien nomads will return and Rohn said to those present this symbol here in our database represents your Earth. Franz Waldheim said the last package that we brought down from the 'New Adventure', space freighter that is still in its package form is in the holding cargo bay in the SHOP No.8 garage and it was never opened and this powerful electromagnetic multiphase pulse laser beam that we can easily be converted from simply a communications tool to a modified high beam weapon we can use against these alien nomads if they were to ever come here on Triton.

Later that Earth day on Triton where Ramon Sanchez and Paul Stewart with Rohn are now outside installing the new modified laser that is now put right next to one of the array multifunction telescopes that will act like a rangefinder aiming scope to provide very accurate beam defense that Jackson Banes will utilize and that he will be provided with the training during the next few Earth days by Anna Magdalena, to carefully operate it on this now built and assembled aiming console. And, now later at Earth dinner time everyone was sitting down enjoying their newly created dish plates of food provided by Arlene cummings, Peter Walker, Mary Walton, and Laura Philmore with help and assistance by 'Rohn', and the fine meal consisted of Artificial grasshopper powder created tofu vegetable (soy) steak, with miniature sweet potato, and miniature broccoli with miniature potatoes with parsley soup, and for desert miniature apple pie with tofu vanilla ice cream with soy milk or beer.

And, after their dinner they sat at the library resting and enjoying tofu blended vodka with fruit juice or homemade craft beer. With, Arlene, Peter, Mary,Laura, and Rohn saying to the rest of the team members that when the 'New Adventure gave us this new multi-biological create processing and replicator device we then were able to create and produce in greater quantity and quality and diversity of food here along with our greenhouse produced gardens, and then Arlene said to everyone how is your steak and beer, and they all said great, this steak is quite delicious and this beer taste just like it was coming from a micro-brewery on Earth,and then she said that our team here will even make it taste better in the next few days.

TRINEP 6-6, spacetime

Franz Waldheim now resting in the library and having a cup of newly created brew tea with tofu (soy milk) and biscuits with newly created strawberry jam looking at his tablet. When a message from Anna Magdalena, came through the Cosmoport intercom and said to him can I see you here in Shop No.5 pod unit please, and he then got up and went to No. 5 unit walking in he was met by Anna, Jackson Banes and Rohn. They said to him we received a communications protocol (morse) signal from Mars deep space orbiting observatory that there is unusual activity slightly over one billion miles from Pluto and at first it's there and the next moment it disappeared, can you from your close-up vantage point on Triton to take a look at this anomaly, and the reason why we called you here at No. 5 Franz Waldheim is that wreckage we found slightly over one thousand miles from here states that simply 2215 printed on this wretched piece of broken metal.

Jackson Banes interrupted the meeting in No.5 pod unit in stating that for the past couple of days I have been looking at this strange phenomena anomaly in deep space approximately one to two billion miles past the orbit of Pluto and Charon, and looking at Franz Waldheim and Anna Magdalena in saying to them that I have no explanation as to what it is, and then said Franz Waldheim well what do you mean Jackson, and he said back to me to begin with two days ago I was looking at this, space rock on what I believe was a traveling comet coming very close to Pluto about two billion miles or so then to my astonishment there was what I believe to be either a saucer or a nomadic moon or asteroid and then leaving the comet I then intensely concentrated on this phenomena and guess what, when I again looked at it with the same coordinance as before it disappeared, thinking nothing of it, because maybe I had hallucinated perhaps with the homemade beer the night before, now thinking hard the day before while looking at my optical remote camera/telescope viewfinder I thought it was me, so I forgot about it until yesterday and looking at this strange white what I believe to be a traveling moon of some kind, there was this saucer or asteroid there again, and this time I took some photos of it while it was still there in looking at it quit intensely and guess what this massive whatever it was simply disappeared and vanished into deep space. Then Frnz Waldheim called in Rohn and Daxor, and they came in and Franz Waldheim explained the situation with them and both said that these aliens has to be the 'Orikata', and Rohn said they are truly reptilian in appearance and highly militarized in training and culture, and they must simply be on a fact finding scouting expedition, and Jackson Banes said to Rohn are these 'Orikata', do they have or use one thousand foot scout ships and he said yes particularly when there galaxy class carrier motherships are a least over ten to fifteen thousand feet in diameter.

Rohn also said with Daxor confirming it that one hundred of your Earth years ago my race the 'Utalu, 'fought a valiant but losing space war with the 'Orikata', who according to our database are highly cruel and evil reptilian looking alien creatures, for in our space war with them we had more spaceships but they had bigger ones with more fire power than we did, and we lost over seventy percent of our spaceships to them. We escaped to the best of our ability in escaping their relenting hostile pursuit of us and the remaining thirty or so something spaceships we had left and then some of us who survived went to another solar system hundreds of your light years away from this star system.

And if they have returned back here, they have come back here to conquer this solar system of yours including your Earth, Mars.and the asteroid belt, not to mention your outer world colonies on Titan, Enceladus, and Europa and of course here on Triton with this settlement base that would be the first to be annihilated including us where these reptilian like aliens will not want us as their prisoners or slaves.

Later that day Rohn was working with Jackson Banes on the deep space imaging console while he was taking a small tea break at the mess hall and meeting Anna Magdalena who was also having a small coffee resting break were discussing the events of the past couple of days, when Rohn looking at the image telescope viewfinder saw in the far off distance seven of these massive one thousand foot diameter saucers and then through the Cosmoport intercom system contacted Banes to come back here to the astronomy No.9 pod unit and Anna Magdalena said you mind if I join you Jackson Banes and he said no please come with me. When Banes and Anna Magdalena came into the Astronomy No.9 unit Rohn showed the video and high resolution pictures of the seven saucers and Jackson Banes said to Rohn good work and then on his tablet showed Anna Magdalena these saucers and she then immediately contacted Franz Waldheim and then he summoned all team member personnel to the mess hall conference room for immediate responses to this astonishing images taken of these seven 'Orikata', spaceships. Before they could leave the astronomy Pod No.9 unit Rohn said to Anna Magdalena and Jackson Banes where is the Mothership?

With everyone now arriving at the mess hall to be briefed and to give hopefully answers about these pictures and videos displayed on the wall mounted screen monitors No. 2 Pod unit.

They all are in total disbelief what they are seeing with everyone not sure what kind of answer they could give to remedy the situation. With Paul Stewart stating we should either send them a computer virus or we should remain quiet and let them pass by Neptune and Triton hoping they would most likely go to battle Earth than waste their fire power on us.

Then Anna Magdalena spoke to everyone and they were now intently listening to her, first thing, this is what I would do, I would move the 'Venture', spacecraft somewhere around Triton in a safe valley and with its built in landing struts and thruster rockets, settle down between these cantaloupe hills I believe Daxor can help you with that, and now keep the 'Meridien', spacecraft overhead us in where they would think that this is our sole method to get back to Earth, second we should take our extreme temperature enclosed emergency tents from 'Venture', and bring it down to the SHOP No.6 subsurface and like an old fashion bomb shelter celler wait it out until they make their move to destroy us on this base or leave us alone, and three we should allow 'Rohn', to show us how to use these ray guns that Franz Waldheim took with him in the now non existent surface spaceship and put safely in storage in Shop No. 8 garage.

And, then Franz Waldheim spoke and said thank you for your realistic response analysis and ideas here Commander Anna Magdalena, and now is their anyone else here to also provide ideas or questions regarding this possible invasion of the inner planets by the 'Orikata', aliens? And, then Joanne Collins interrupted the others in saying we are here as a civilian scientist and not the military or warriors to do battle on Triton with probably an advanced alien race of soldiers that know how to kill, and we should somehow try to contact them and say to them we come and are here in peace, and then Rohn and Daxor said to Joanne Collins and the rest of them that these neo-reptilian aliens are truly warriors and military soldiers that would gladly kill you as part of their culture and their society. At the end of the meeting Franz Waldheim announced to everyone we are going to vote on this resolution in favor of either Anna Magdaleas resolution for war or Joanne Collins resolution for peace, with. Ayes going to Anna or nays going to Joanne,now we will spend five minutes in silence and then vote and I will at first remain neutral, but I will then go and give my 100% support with the larger vote.

It has now been five minutes and going clockwise around the mess hall conference table the first one is <u>Paul Stewart, who says aye</u>, then next to him is <u>Arlene Cummings who says nay,</u> then after her is <u>Jeniffer Aldridge who says aye</u>, after her is <u>Ramon Sanchez who says aye</u>, and after him is <u>Peter Walker who says nay</u>, and then after him is <u>Mary Walton who says nay,</u> and after her is <u>Anna Magdalena who says aye,</u> and then after her is <u>Laura Philmore who says nay</u>, and now after her is <u>Jackson Banes who says aye</u> and now after him is <u>Joanne Collins who said nay</u> and then after her is <u>Jeffery Watkins who said aye</u> and after him is <u>Allison Beils who said aye</u> and then <u>Daxor said aye</u> and <u>Rohn said aye</u> and then <u>Franz Waldheim who said aye</u> and then he counted the votes with ten ayes and five nays and then he said the **ayes** have it and I now fully support the ayes 100% and with it, and now ladies and gentlemen we are now going to war here on Triton.

TRINEP 1-7, spacetime

After a very good breakfast at 0700 hours Earth morning time the team members are now hard at work preparing in hoping to never see their new enemy the 'Orikata', from coming here to our Cosmoport base, with Anna Magdalena, Paul Stewart and Daxor taking off for the 'Venture', spacecraft and Rohn teaching Franz Waldheim, Ramon and Alison beils how to use the seven ray guns and five ray rifles with auto-finder scope and display attachments and Rohn saying to Franz Waldheim I am glad you took the charger units of these weapons with you because without it we can not use it after our initial testing round is finished, and he said I knew that and also I took these blinding intense bright light flash units that can be attached on each ray weapon. The team of Magdalena, Stewart and Daxor took off from Cosmoport base and went to the space capsule landing bay of the 'venture', spacecraft and immediately went to the bridge and in less than half an hour they blasted off from their orbit of Triton and following Daxor instructions and went to a very secluded part of Triton and with their landing thrusters and struts unfolded, and now open they landed with their retro-rockets to a soft landing in a valley ravine that is big enough for the spacecraft with a flat hard surface and once down they made sure that everything was secure systems in an off mode with the exception of the four AX5 thorium reactor batteries that is never turned off, then they left from the space capsule pod landing bay and blasted off for the return trip back to cosmoport base. And,once they arrived at the Cosmoport base SHOP No.8 pod garage unit they found Franz Waldheim teaching judo and jiu jitsu to the others as part of to toughen them up and allowing them to equal their defense training against the 'Orikata', neo-reptilian aliens.

Their training lasted most of the entire Earth day, and only allowing a few moments of rest and coffee and tea breaks. When Anna Magdalena and Paul Stewart and Daxor joined the others in the SHOP no.8 garage now used as a mini training center, Anna and Paul said can I help out and Franz Waldheim said that according to your personnel files both of you are trained martial arts experts and with your prior defense training can you help out and teach the others in your self defense skills, they both said of course we can help out, and Anna and Paul said who is next here.

The next day at Cosmoport base, at breakfast with everyone was tired and exhausted from the day before exercises and defense training now are sitting at the mess hall table with home made corn flakes with strawberries and tofu (soy) milk and coffee and tea. One hour later Anna Magdalena, Paul Stewart, Daxor and with Jackson Banes who is able to move slowly because of his defense training, at SHOP No. 9 Astronomy unit is now listening in on an unusual broadcast from far out in space past Pluto and Charon orbits and this unusual communication audio sound that Daxor with his vast database found when he was at the now non existent frozen entrapped spacecraft console unit and what his robotic excellent translation algorithm ability has pieced together, is that they are about to make their presence known to us and we very soon are ready to show our supreme might and who we truly are. The message has now been recorded and heard by Franz Waldheim who like Banes is walking slowly into the SHOP No. 8 astronomy unit and then he said to Anna Magdalena we have now been contacted by the 'Orikata', neo-reptilian creatures who may come to this solar system and once here will soon be headed toll Earth, can you please now send this rebroadcast coded information and scrambled and in morse code to Earth, and she said yes, I will go now to the No. 5 communications unit and send the message immediately.

Then Franz Waldheim spoke to his team members and said to them that we have to start construction of our submersible habitat survival shelter heavy duty tent and then said to his team we have to have enough supplies to last for several and they all listened to him and then they started the construction. With work underway they started to create simplified foods in their food processing bio-machine, like high protein snacks and flavored water tasting vitamin and mineral drinks to last several days down their. Then they put additional lights at the water pond leading to the vertical hole and man cover hatch door,then they put a man cover hatch door with a combination lock on its door and a video camera in the corner of the SHOP No. 6 mining unit that would record who comes in and looks at the new and locked man cover hatch door. Then later that day at dinner time they were all sitting at the conference/menu food table and Franz Waldheim then said to all before we eat our food is their anything we could do more to escape these neo-reptilian beings and all of them said perhaps we could.

Later that day their work was half done underneath with the last of the specialized pressurized tents slowly being completed and now at 1800 hours are having dinner and speaking about what would happen if they came here at Cosmoport. And, Franz Walheim said all of you will go down while I stay up here along with Daxor who can act as my interpreter up here being by my side with me in my discussion with these aliens that your lives here in the subterranean world on Triton hopefully will save you all from the wrath of these neo-reptilians. With everyone listening to Franz Waldheim at their dinner table enjoying their meal and Anna Magdalena spoke for the group it would be hard to leave you and Daxor to the aliens and what we know of them they will kill you,everyone concurred with her that we really should stay together and try to defeat these neo-reptilian aliens.

TRINEP 3-7, spacetime

The next morning at breakfast the team members sitting at the table were they were in a somber.mood, where they will have to complete the last of the pressurized tent down below, and with Ramon Sanchez and Jeffery Watkins with Paul Stewart Helping out, they were now putting in place the electrical wiring units that will funnel conduit power from the thorium reactors to the pressurized tents and would also automatically power every aspect of the base with their remote control computer tablet unit for up to one Earth month without human intervention and without hopefully any alien knowledge they were doing so while they were secluded safely down below.

Franz Waldheim then said in looking around at everybody at the table that at least for a little while this outpost of humanity made this solar system capable of this moon, Titan our ability to explore and survive this extreme frigid elements this moon can throw at us and by our human race team we have survived and thrived, and with all our knowledge that by simply being here we must explore space, this is our heritage and calling here next to the last final frontier of this solar system and somehow we will win this because we have to and it begins here on Triton.

Everyone then clapped and said well done to Franz Waldheim and for a little while they felt good to have their hopefully not their last meal, now their breakfast has begun. Their morning meal was mostly created with our scientific biological and horticural team members, that they have genetically produced (tofu) soybeans created in the garden greenhouse pods and it consisted of miniature created garden orange juice Tofu (soy) beacon or tofu (soy) sausages with tofu (soy) synthetic produced eggs and tofu (soy) created cornbread and or tofu style (soy) toasted garden wheat bread slices served with fresh strawberry or blackberry jam and served with coffee or tea. And, an hour later they were hard worked completely in their tasks and everyone was going to finish at the end of this day.

TRINEP 4-7, spacetime

The start of a new day and right after breakfast the entire team members including Daxor and Rohn working with Jackson Banes, were back at their hard work in their individual SHOP Pod units and Franz Waldheim inspecting the subterranean habitat tent down below and find the tent ready to receive the team members when called for to evacuate the surface and while down below decided to take a walk around the dark eight to fifteen foot world and using his tablet computer noticed a slight breeze coming from one of the walls with a small vented hole and looking into this small hole saw another cave beyond this hole and decided to contact Ramon Sanchez and Paul Stewart to come down with gigging tools and when they came down and met Franz Waldheim started to dig and then from a small hole into a six foot wide entrance and then they decided to enter and looked inside this new cave that after a few minutes in walking through and saw these incredible multicolored biolumence crystals on the cave walls that go on many hundreds of yards.

And then Franz Waldheim looking down on the ground that they were walking on with his high beam flashlight aimed his chemical analyzer geological tablet computer and found that this grounis is mainly made up of silica SIO2 or silicon dioxide with other small elements of (soil aluminum, calcium, magnesium, potassium and iron) as silicate compounds and saying to Paul and Ramon we will have to come back here later this afternoon Earth time, and this time we will be prepared for a long hike in this newly discovered cave corridor.for potential future mining potential down here in this cave.

Later after lunch the new team carrying wheeled four large gallon size containers came down and went through the new cave entrance hole and went into the cave corridor looking down at their feet and the cave walls with these bioluminescence multicolored crystals on the cave walls. The new teams is Peter Walker, Joanne Collins, Franz Waldheim, Paul Stewart, and Anna Magdalena are now scraping off the walls of these multicolored crystal mines and scooping up near the cave walls the ground soil and its Silica compounds in putting it in those containers and helping them loading them in the vertical hole to go up to their SHOP units.

And, then Franz Waldheim. Paul Stewart and Anna Magdalena went back into the new cave and went through that cave corridor and then walking over one mile they checked their oxygen levels and battery power supply that was more than half way into the green safe mode, and then they said being very tired to Franz Waldheim if you want to go further on we will follow you and then Waldheim said let us go one more mile and then we will go back to the vertical hole. They then agreed and went further along in this strange underground cave with thousands of these glowing bioluminescent shining crystallines with their multicolored flashing stones somewhat and then not a half a mile further on they stopped and then they looked in complete awe for in front of them was this immense underground chasm were they were standing over ten stories above on this over extended terrace on this chasm world in measuring five miles in front of them by seven miles in width and five stories above them on their standing terrace.

And, then walking around the terrace, Anna Magdalena saw next to the terrace wall a kind of naturally made stairs in going down three stories and she told Franz Waldheim and Paul Stewart she was going down and they saw her going down the natural starway and at three stories down she found another cave entrance this time there was no biolumenance crystals anywhere it was completely dark, and she then decided not to go into the dark cave, she then summoned Franz and Paul to come walk down carefully and when they did they were now seeing this mysterious dark cave where they were standing in front of this cave entrance where they were very intrigued to where this cave will go to. With Franz Waldheim saying maybe tomorrow we will come back here and explore this dark cave fuller. but Franz Waldheim said now we have to go back because our oxygen and power levels are approaching low and reading red and we have to go back to the vertical hole and back to Cosmoport base.

TRINEP 5-7, spacetime

The next day at breakfast sitting at the table was Arlene Cummings Mary Walton Joanne Collins and Peter Walker announced to everyone and with Franz Waldheim listening that yesterday when we brought up these geological soil samples and put it into the chemical analyzer its chemical components showed an extremely soil base to work with and found it to be very rich in what we could now do here at Cosmoport and to finally create a greenhouse food supply that is more natural and varied in what we can produce here on Triton, said Joanne Collins as the lead speaker of the group. Now finishing their breakfast the engineering group said not only the greenhouse will prosper but we now can create light bulbs also in where we can have light here almost forever said Ramon Sanchez and with back up from Jeffery Watkins and Joan Collins who said these biolumenance multicolored christalines are truly incredible that these are strictly inanimate minerals and appears not to be of any life form whats so ever, the amount of light they are able to produce are anywhere from 40 watts to 60 watts of light that are incredible in being constant light that are willing to last almost for a very long time.

Jackson Banes and Daxor with Rohn are together looking hard at Cosmoport multifunction telescopes and two dish antennas that are now chiefly aimed at deep space past pluto and Charon in trying to somehow eavesdrop and spy on these neo-reptilian aliens in what their objectives are in whether their intentions will bring their invasion to this solar system and Triton and for now there is no sign that they are making any move at all.

TRINEP 6-7, spacetime

The next day at Cosmoport, at their breakfast table, there were the last of the tofu breakfast menu because as of tomorrow there will be fresher and even a better tasting food, but for now the usual pancakes,with egg and sausages and toast with blueberry jam and coffee or tea, most of it tofu (soybean) based in origin. Then afterwards at work in the greenhouse laboratories they, Arlene Cummings, Peter Walker, Mary Walton, Laura Philmore and Joan Collins are now bio-engineering thanks to the new soil they found in the new cave down below and put into effect in its biochemical processor and sequence generator that will create even more Earth like food for our table settings.

Franz Waldheim then speaking to Jackson Banes, said to him you are finding nothing new out there in deep space while having freshly made scones with blueberry jam and coffee for franz and tea for Jackson. And, he said back to Franz no and that I will say privately to you that this is quite disconcerting and creates a scenario for an unannounced quick attack here at Cosmoport base, and I think sometime this afternoon he said to Franz Waldheim that we should have an emergency survival drill and analyze the time it will take us in how long we will take to go down to our survival tent. Then Franz Waldheim listening carefully to what Jackson said and nodded to him, yes, you are quite right and then on the Cosmoport base intercom said to everyone that at 4:00 pm Earth time we are going to have a special survival drill and it is now 2:00 pm Earth time and everyone will you please get ready to move down below.

Precisely at 4:00 pm the survival test drill that was called for took too long and were if actually they had to escape the neo-reptilian aliens would have lost and potentially been killed in going down to the survival tent. Then Franz Waldheim said to the team members first thing at 8:00 am Earth time we will be doing this test again and tonight think about what everyone of you can do to speed up your survival results. But now rest up for tomorrow and have some dinner and rest afterwards.

TRINEP 1-8, spacetime

The next day at Cosmoport after 8:00 am they redid the survival test and everyone did much better and was within the ballpark time necessary in achieving a quick escape to the subterranean survival tent below and Franz Waldheim was very pleased and he said by 4:00 pm we will do another for now the last test and he said if you can meet the same test results then we are ready for our survival when these neo-reptilian creature invaders come here to Cosmoport base. While they wait for 4:00 pm, Franz Waldheim and Paul Stewart and with Anna Magdalena, went down and stood in front of the newly made cave entrance and adjusting their high beam flashlights looking at each other in their space suits helmet visors and please check your oxygen and power supply that we can spend at least two hours once we go that chasm through this new cave..

Then they entered the new cave entrance and went to that chasm and walked down below three stories to that darken cave and standing in front of the cave entrance they said this is it and can you please check your oxygen and power supply for the last time so that we can stay and they then replied back all is okay for our one hour stay here. And now they walked into the cave and what they saw was a cave that was devoid of anything except the blackness of rocks and nothing more, then this narrow cave was slowly getting bigger and widening as we walked and Franz Waldheim speaking to Paul Stewart and Anna Magdalena said we will continue for another half mile here if nothing happens we will go back, and then something strange happened when they went one hundred feet more than they had to stop because in front of them was this very smooth pure black wall that was ten feet high by something like fifty feet wide, the entire width of the cave with Anna Magdalena then touching it and then this wall lighted up into a light blue shining almost like a glass or ice blue wall and after a few moments it was all black again, then Anna touched the black wall again and it turned lighted shining blue again and this time she touched it again and her hand went right through it but she then retrieved the hand and again she put her hand right through it but this time she went right through it and Franz then Waldheim and Paul Stewart had no choice but to follow her and they went straight through and when they came out on the other side of this lighted blue wall and they were now in a strange and unbelievable place like a world where there was these neo-reptilian aliens 'Orikata', all about them walking about and talking to each other what appears to be a family walking outings.

But then when Anna Magdalena tried to speak to one of them they could not see her or communicate with her at all for they could not see the three of them like they were non-existent transparent dimensional ghost's. What they were seeing was these 'Orikata', society alien beings enjoying their daily lifestyle without a worry or care in an incredible ultra-modern city on this strange world with two suns, and now she looks ahead and sees this alien looking at her as this alien can see her and Franz and Paul, who also noticed this alien looking at them and then this strange looking cat like (cheetah animal) came to her and tried to be petted by Anna but she could not touch the animal but then the alien called the animal back and the alien and the cat-like creature went inside this circle teleportation transportation ring gateway device and left to go into somewhere and then Franz Waldheim and Paul stewart and Anna Magdalena simply walked about this strange future city like world in seeing its advanced architecture and this future teleportation circle ring transportation device looking at people go into it and coming out of it from one place to another on this strange world what appears to be a fascinating place by these neo-reptilian advanced creatures said Anna to Paul and Franz.

Then Franz Waldheim told Paul Stewart and Anna Magdalena that we have to leave here because our oxygen and power supply is going into the red zone, and when they went back to the wall where they came from and touched the wall all of a sudden this neo-reptilian world disappeared and when they turned around it was an empty blue lighted cube of fifty feet by fifty feet by ten feet high ceiling and with its flooring that was a mysterious kind of a metallic ceramic alloy feel and shining look.

They then said to one another that this maybe a special artificially created hologram for anyone who comes here and then Anna Magdalena then touched the wall again and she was now able to put her hand and arm right through it in saying to Franz and Paul please follow me and they did and then they came out of this strange what Anna called an insight of these alien creatures who created their world through this incredible hologram but she wanted to know why is this here on Triton and the other two Franz and Paul did not know, and then they were out in the total darkness of the cave and Franz said to Paul and Anna let us go back to our world at our surface Cosmoport base and then they left walking out of the cave and going out of the chasm and back to the new cave entrance and back to the vertical hole and up to their Cosmoport base for some reflection and coffee at the mess hall said Franz Waldheim to Anna and Paul who agreed in saying yes to that.

Coming back to Cosmoport base, it is now ten to four o'clock and Franz Waldheim with help from Paul Stewart and Anna Magdalena then conducted and supervised their survival drill and sure enough they turned out their best performance yet in achieving a quick and immediate rescue and eviction into the vertical tunnel down into their survival tent, and then Franz Waldheim said we are completely ready when these neo-reptilian aliens would want to come here. And then Franz Waldheim said tomorrow afternoon at exactly 2:00 pm Earth time we are going to have our weapons training exercises and combat shooting skill set drills with Ramon Sanchez providing us with his newly created and improvised and modified weapons for our defense against these neo-reptilian alien invaders.

TRINEP 2-8, spacetime

It is now the next day on this very cold and frigid moon, Triton. They are amount to in the next two hours develop their skill set shooting and training sessions with several weapons that would be located in the SHOP No.8 garage unit that would be used in today's training in their aiming and shooting abilities and will be supervised by Ramon Sanchez who is a trained weapons expert back on Earth. But first comes their breakfast which will be consisted of, bio-replica made wheat pancakes, new improved (tofu) soy eggs, (soy) sausage and freshly garden produced squeezed orange juice with whole wheat bread toast with strawberry jam from garden and coffee or tea.

In the SHOP No. 8 garage unit they all came and on the table that Ramon set up and co-supervised by Anna Magdalena and Paul Stewart, they one by one aimed, cocked and fired their weapon at a specially made blast resistant ceramic alloy target board created by Joanne Collins and Ramon Sanchez, in the afternoon the day before. With one by one taking their weapon of choice the fired with aiming help from Anna and Paul at that target board and most of the team members scored well if not great, with Franz Waldheim scoring the least, with his excuse in saying i am a scientist not a foot soldier, but Anna Magdalena said do not worry I will help you and will improve your aiming abilities. Later that day at SHOP No.9 astronomy unit Jackson Banes received a message from deep space past Pluto and Charon and the message said,

'We are coming and you will prepare for our invasion on your moon'.

Then the message stopped and then Jackson Banes gave the message to Franz Waldheim, Anna Magdalena and Paul Stewart for evaluation and response.

While Franz Waldheim is pondering as to what to make of this message, he has given the go ahead and allowed Peter Walker, Joanne Collins and Rohn to go and explore beyond the chasm and will allow Anna Magdalena later to follow and communicate with them if they get into any trouble. The new team of explorers, Joanne, Peter and Rohn in one hours time have left Cosmoport and fully equipped and supplied with air and power for up to five hours, left and went through the new cave entrance and almost hiking went to the chasm terrace and going down those three story steps and finding a small down sloping walkway on the cliff wall of this mountain hill past the last steps of the dark cave entrance, they then went down to this narrow ravine to its floor walking and if possible taking pictures with their high beam helmet hats and flashlights they then noticed they walked over one mile from those steps leading down from the terrace and then they came across a small tributary like river and they followed it on to its narrow embankments and then they stopped.

For now in front of them was an incredible sight that they have never seen before, what they were looking at was an ocean view in front of them but that was not the amazing part, when they looked up towards the ceiling of this ocean, it was extreme water (H2O) according to their chemical analyzer tablet this frozen ice was going many thousands of thousands of feet in any direction and some of the frozen ice water was coming down to perhaps as low as fifteen feet above this ocean like water world according to their helmet 500mm zoom night scope measuring attachment cameras. They then shone their high beam lights on to the water and it was absolutely crystal clear with the lighted water going down more than one hundred feet. What amazed them most because of the very low gravity here on Triton, this ocean like body of water had a surreal slow motion effect with the waves and crested ripples hitting this above five feet shoreline.

Then being very careful they went down the embankment shoreline and took several samples of the soils and ice water and took it with them back to Cosmoport base to further analyze it, as they were walking back they noticed that looking above them the frozen ice ceiling that above them turned to rock and they knew they were past the shoreline going into the underground subsurface of Triton and while walking back they noticed on the one embankment side of the ice water tributary river was a glowing and moving plant like creature resembling a jellyfish but with it having roots into the oozing scum like soil which they took a sample of, and then they looked at its unique almost see through greenish skin flesh and they shined it with their high beam flashlights and it quickly curled up into a protective round glove then lowering their high beams the creature came back out of its round glove and then they took several pictures of this living creature on Triton.

And then, Peter walker said why didn't we see them before, and Joanne Collins said because our high beam flashlights were on while we were walking they must have curled up into their round glove when we came near them, and as a result, these creatures were not showing themselves to us as we walked by, and then they decided not to touch it or take it back with them for now, but with these photos we will show to Franz Waldein, and they then continued to move on and seeing lights in the near distance at the terrace stairways they said to each other that it must be Anna Magdalena waiting for us to come, and finally coming back out of the chasm and walking up the stairway to the terrace and there was meeting them, Anna Magdalena who was waiting for them while she was looking at their lights coming near her in the distance, and she said to them how was your walk they said it was incredible and then they left together to go back to the surface at Cosmoport base.

Back now at Cosmoport base the trio of Joanne Collins, Peter Walker and Rohn were analyzing there find and showing Franz Waldheim and Paul Stewart and Anna Magdalena, what they have discovered and they were completely amazed and almost ecstatic that there is this simple jelly fish like plant of lifeform here on Triton. Later in the laboratory SHOP No.4 chemical facility that was transformed into a biological research and food center and development unit, they Joanne Collins, Mary Walton, Peter Walker and Rohn brought in these river bank samples of soil and goo from where the jellyfish was naturally planted and thriving and by using simplified forensics of this mush material Mary Walton called this sample she said to all that they have discovered that this mush like goo that has complex protein structures, with multiple mineral component properties with a living simple one floating cellular enzymes of plant and animal eukaryotic Vacuole and Lysosomes cells that are alive and bonding with a light emitting pigment, the luciferase enzyme and also a singular protein called ricin with aconitine proteins that bonds to one another and right in front of them in this lab they see these one cells bonding to other cellular mitochondria cells and forming new complex multicellular organisms. From this mush goo soil and we would expect that in two or three Earth days they would be forming and maturing buds of these micro-creatures into bioluminescent jellyfish like plants.

The next Triton morning at the Cosmoport base, again they are having a splendid breakfast and Franz Waldheim speaking to the scientific group looking into the soil near the ocean on the side of the embankment and with those bizarre and curious jellyfish plants and their response they gave back to Franz Waldheim was simply amazing, with Mary Walton and assisted by Laura Philmore and Daxor, they both said they have never seen this kind of life form ever in this solar system, they viewed the videos and closeup high definition pictures of these creatures, and they asked ourselves in the lab what is their jellyfish plants story, and now we ask you Franz Waldheim in how did these creatures come here to Triton and we both agreed along with Daxor that they are not from this moon.

Then Anna Magdalena kindly interrupted the conversation and said to them there is only one plausible explanation and that both of you remember Franz and Paul when we were inside this what we call a hologram being in there world, but what if it wasn't a hologram but the real thing, that somehow we were teleported to their world, Then Franz and Paul together said that can't possibly be for no one except this alien and his cat like creature saw us but no one else did and then they said there were a lot of these other neo-reptilian aliens simply walking by and not one of them noticed us, and then she said this is a mystery for now I can't answer you both back.

Later that morning Jackson Banes was looking at his data and the solar system photographic pictures from Nereid asteroid moon of Neptune and saw something ominous and dreadful there was fifteen huge space saucers head to the inner planets and they were leaving Neptune's orbit and they are traveling at least over two hundred thousand miles per hour when he saw this he immediately contacted Franz Waldheim on the network Cosmoport intercom and told him the horrible news of an invasion coming to Earth. Then Franz Waldheim immediately gathered everyone to an emergency meeting in the mess hall and Jackson Banes brought proof with data and pictures and now Franz Waldheim said to everyone lock and load your weapon of choice, looks like we may see the aliens very soon here. Everyone here do you have any questions regarding this alien invasion and they were all mum being horrified that within weeks Earth will be invaded by these huge ships, and then Franz Waldheim said to Anna Magdalena to immediately contact Earth Space Command and tell them to prepare for an invasion in scrambled morse code,please and she got up and went to SHOP No.5 communications unit and sent the message to Space Command on the Moon where they relay it to Earth. One Earth hour later they all retrieved their weapons of choice and were ready to defeat these aliens when they come here.

It has now been four hours and not one alien has shown up and Franz Waldheim has contacted Jackson Banes in his Astronomy unit No.9 and he said back to Franz there is absolutely nothing in space with anything resembling an invasion here by their huge saucer starships. It is now six hours later and Jackson Banes said nothing is in near space of Triton. And then Anna Magdalena spoke to Franz Waldheim and repeated to him that there has to be a reason that they have not invaded here at Cosmoport base, and again she said to him that this stranger and cat creature looking at us and me trying to pet the aliens cat has got to be their reason for not attacking here, and with Franz Waldheim at wits end looking at her and said there is no other reason that I could explain that twelve hours ago these neo-reptilian aliens left for Earth and not one attack has incurred here, but in the next one hour if nothing happens here I will say to you that I believe you.

It has now been fifteen hours since the invasion has begun and Anna Magdalena as communications officer has been contacted by Earth and they communicated back to her what invasion? What are you guys on? You do know the rules that there are no drugs to use on Triton in your working for Earth as directed by Space Command for the outerworlds, when you have something to actually contact us with then please communicate back to us thank you and end of transmission.

Then Franz Waldheim called for an immediate conference at the mess hall table and everyone has attended and then Jackson Banes speaking to the others, said perhaps they called it off for some unknown reason, what do you mean said Franz in speaking to Jackson perhaps like our training with our weapons they were doing their own mock attacks in their training perhaps using their advanced alien communications equipment in eavesdropping on our solar system transmissions in telling them that Earth for now is too powerful for them and decided to call it off and then maybe in the near future they will have more and perhaps bigger starships to eventually defeat Earth, with everybody attending and agreeing with Jackson and with Anna Magdalena in saying it makes perfect sense to me and the other team members agreeing with her.

TRINEP 4-8, spacetime

It is now the next day on Triton and Anna Magdalena and Paul Stewart at 0600 hours Earth time they went into Franz Waldheim's small cubicle office in the SHOP No.1 resting unit and he was their early before breakfast while looking at this data and photographic pictures that Jackson Banes gave him, before he starts the day at his geological SHOP No.3 unit, and walking in unannounced was Anna and Paul, and Franz Waldheim looking up said to them can I help you two, and then they said right away we have to go back to that chasm stairway dark cave and go back into that hologram and somehow find a way to communicate with them on their future intentions towards this solar system and the both of them looking quite serious at him and said that you have to come with us or without us and then Franz Waldheim smiled at them and he fully agreed with them and said to them I will go with you and he then told them only after a good and hearty breakfast in one hour, and we will start to go back there at 0800 hours Earth time.

After their breakfast Franz Waldheim, Paul Stewart and Anna Magdalena left Cosmoport and went to the chasm and walking down those natural stairways they came to the dark cave entrance and they walked in and going to where they first encountered the wall there was nothing they shined their high beams flashlights to where the hologram should have been walking into the space now left vacant and bare with nothing here except rocks, with Franz, Paul and Anna what is happening here where is this wall Paul said and looking around on the one side of the wall to the other side side of the wall, Anna Saw with her searchlights a piece of metal from the hologram wall on the ground and put it into her satchel bag and Franz Waldheim said to Anna Magdalena you were very right this not a hologram but a space portal gateway that we just came across in our earlier outing here. And, then they left to go back to Cosmoport base on the surface, as they were walking up the stairway they noticed that the chasm was slowly filling up with cold ice water and then seeing this Franz said to Anna and Paul we must hurry to get out of here or we will drown here so please walk and hop if you can and leave here now and they did and when they stopped briefly at the terrace they could see that this ocean is covering the chasm with ice cold Triton water. They left walking quite fast and they realized that the water properly stopped just shy of the terrace with everything under that covered, and their chances to communicate with these neo-reptilians 'Orikata', aliens are now over. And, when they returned back to their Cosmoport base Communications unit No.5 they were now tired and disappointed that we did not try to communicate with them earlier and while sitting down and resting,

Anna Magdalena then had a very clever idea she presented to Franz and Paul, that involves putting the scrap wall metal she found and somehow develop a way to send a communication message to them through this metal fragment somehow, with Franz and Paul saying to her good luck and they then got up and left No.5 unit to go back to their individual

SHOP units but first said Franz I am having a cup of tea in the mess hall kitchen and Paul said to him make that two cups of tea and Anna now smiling at them leaving her to work out a way to somehow use this scrap metal as a conduit to communicate with these aliens.

Later that Earth day in the afternoon Anna went to Daxor and Rohn and said to them, can you help me with a project and the said sure we will help you and they followed Anna to the No.5 communications unit small lab section and she said to them that I need your electronic and alien expertise for you and I to figure a way to communicate with these aliens with Daxor somewhat egear and Rohn saying why do you want to communicate with them when according to your Earth Space Command there was no attack on their world, and Anna said to them besides you Rohn if we can communicate with these aliens they may be able to show us the way to travel to other star systems and with other advances they can help us with, and rohn said I understand will help you try to communicate with the 'Orikata', alien neo-reptilian race.

They worked for four hours on Anna Magdalena's project with no results of any kind so far, for they tried everything possible in using the scrap metal as a conduit for her in trying to communicate with these aliens, and then Jackson Banes walks in and simply saying hello and said to her how is it going and she said back to him not so good, and he then said can I just sit down on that stool over there for a few minutes drinking my tea and she said sure, why not while she and Daxor with Rohn are putting every conceivable electronic attached unit to that scrap metal, and then he made a brief observation to her with Daxor and Rohn listening in, you said that when you first got there this hologram portal was there, and when you came back it was gone, and you brought up an excellent theory that it was not a hologram but an actual interdimensional gateway portal, is that right Anna Magdalena, and she said back to Banes yes that's what I said two days ago. Well said banes I also have this strange far out idea that I want to say to you, and your colleagues over there, my idea is why don't you simply create a field generated interdimensional communications emitter field that is connected to that scrap metal that as you said can be used like a key or conduit to reach out to them, by using my deep space antenna that you are wasting time with when I can easily convert it to a deep space portal that would easily create a hologram portal but this one you will be able to communicate these aliens with.

And then Anna looking at Banes almost happy and astonished said I thank you very much, because what you just said Banes makes perfect sense to me, and then she said to Daxor and Rohn who were standing and listening to this conversation, and then she said to them this is what we have to do know and then Jackson Banes smiling at them got up from the stool and said to them that dinner is in one hour Earth time, and he left to go back to his SHOP astronomy No.9 unit to now make preparations for her to send the interdimensional field generation communication signal to the aliens by way of his revved up power dish antenna. Then in half an hour Anna Magdalena, Daxor and Rohn created their interdimensional communications emitter field. This time they tweaked the emitter with a micro phased multi-wobble (one billion vibrations to 20 billion vibrations per one random second per second time) lasting for a continues one hour intervals with different band widths from very narrow to extremely wide in being sent through the dish antenna aimed at beyond Pluto and Charon. Then Anna said to Daxor can spend one hour here to monitor the results in the communications unit and in the astronomy unit and then Daxor said yes I will be here Anna Magdalena.

And, then she said thank you and we will be right back and she left with Rohn for dinner at the mess hall. While they were at dinner Daxor not twenty minutes waiting for something to happen here at communication pod unit has now received a message from the aliens and it said that the great 'Orikata', now will not invade your solar system, but it is our intention to be peaceful and very soon we will be in contact again with your human kind. Then Daxor was from the beginning of the incoming message was then recording this message from the 'Orikata', neo-reptilian alien creatures and will give that message to Anna when she comes back here.

When Anna Magdalena, Jackson Banes an Rohn came back from their dinner, Daxor gave the message to Anna, Jackson and Rohn and then Anna gave the message to Franz Waldheim and he said to Anna keep on communicating with them and perhaps to arrange a meeting with them, if it can be possible and then Anna went back to Jackson Daxor and Rohn and said we have to again try to reach them. Well they created the same communications link as before with Jackson and Anna Magdalena, Daxor and Rohn and they decided to leave the multifunction phased and multi-wobble width band frequency open, but then Jackson said our dish cannot drain power for too long here when we might need power elsewhere.

Then they decided to leave it alone for now and in one hour if they could not contact them we will try again in the morning, and Anna agreed to that call by Jackson Banes. And, then Daxor interrupted Jackso and Anna in saying your frequency setting is to low it should be 952.768 terahertz and they looked at their reading and Anna said, I set it at 137.560 and then Daxor said it was to low for a proper bandwidth electromagnetic spectrum result and Jackson said I believe Daxor is right, and then she set the digital reading at the higher 952.768. Well Jackson said to Anna I am going to bed and read about the great space explorers of twenty-first century, good night everyone and then he said have Daxor stand watch for anything coming in and she looking at Daxor said yes. Then at about 10:35 pm that Earth night time onTriton they almost woke up simultaneously when they got up they went to the mess hall and made their coffee and tea, sitting at the small but capable kitchen four seat table they spoke to each other and said are you thinking what I am thinking and Anna said to Jackson you go first and he said these alien neo-reptilian creatures right now do not exist, and she said go on, and then he said sometime in the past they must have for whatever reason come to this solar system and she said to him bingo, you are quite right Jackson, what we are doing almost defies the laws of science by contacting these aliens not now but when in the past that we have to figure out,

And just then Daxor came in and said you have to follow me to the communications unit, and got up and went and when they arrived they were contacting us and immediately Jackson took over and said to them where are you, we are in the yellow sun and orbiting this blue green ice world and where are you, we want to speak with you, with the help of Daxor he was able to provide the tweaking of the universal translator computer unit in their last contact with us. And, then Anna told them what happened with you in your future we had to leave when our comrades came for us and then we left your solar system but how do know this and where are you, and Jackson said to her quietly don't say anything and then she said I will somehow contact you again tomorrow and then Jackson turned off quickly the machine and also by remote turned off the dish antenna from anymore time portal communication searches by these aliens.

And, Rohn said to Jackson and Anna why did you turn off the machine and the dish antenna so fast, because Jackson said to him what we do not know is where they are possibly from in the near but distant past historically what we do not want them to know is where our time communications signal is coming from and also, to Rohn we do not know how advanced they are and if they have any capability of space-time travel into the future and in particular our future.

I have one question for you Jackson and that is the cubic hologram world that myself. Franz and Paul went through, that us was quite real and he said back to Anna, I know and he said it may be a gateway portal but then when you went again Anna for the second time there it was completely gone except for this crap metal you found at that wall and then Jackson said to her that hologram you went through was a mistake on their part they could not figure how you and Franz were able to be here on Triton and for you three to walk right into their world

I have a theory and I may not be able to prove it but Anna they know who we are and what century we are in and when they destroyed there hologram portal It was for one reason only they knew we are the human race that have now become very advanced and they somehow know that we are experimenting with time-space travel and how it works and they thought we would be able to go back in time and prevent them from these alien beings from coming and staying here in our solar system, and that is why your hologram cube was destroyed to remove any doubt from their alien point of view for gaining the technology by us in going back to the near distant past.

Jackson in saying to her that this scrap metal you hope to somehow communicate with these neo-reptilian aliens will never happen they are somehow afraid of us, as we are afraid of them, they have no intentions coming here in peace and what I think is that this solar system is better off being owned and colonized by humans, and not far away alien races that mean harm to us, because this is our future and after this speech to you Anna Magdalena and Daxor and ROHN, that I would like to say good night to all of you and I will see you all in the morning.

TRINEP 5-8, spacetime

The next morning at breakfast the entire team was enjoying their morning meal and Franz Waldheim said to Jackson and Anna how did it go yesterday and Anna Spoke and said their may be no invasion here in the solar system, everybody was pleasantly very happy as well a Franz who said back to them I believe there intentions in this space-present was non-existent what we were doing is communicating with them in the near distant past and they according to me and Jackson there will be no invasion by the 'Orikata', any time soon, and with much appreciation I as commander and Administrator of this Cosmoport base thank you and the rest of the team from the bottom of our hearts to you and said thank personaly to you to Jackson Banes and Anna Magdalena, and they said don't forget our team crew members Daxor and Rohn who also help us with this project and all of them said thank you again, now also cheering and toasting them with either their coffee or tea.

Later that day Franz Waldheim decided to use the survival tents as a health spa and at the same time to fix the new cave created entrance hole and to ensure that nothing would come through it. While team members will soon begin work and in the meantime in the Astronomy No.9 pod unit Jackson Banes later that day said by private two person intercom said to Franz Waldheim that everything is okay here and at Nereid orbiting the moon with nothing but the emptiness of space. But then puzzled, he said to Franz Waldheim when the first Nereid pictures showed these saucer spacecraft going to the inner planets we had not set up our communication space-time system, and I say to you again how was it possible that they, these huge saucers were physically there going to the inner planets. Frana Waldheim said I do not know but then he said that if everything is okay now try not to worry about what ifs or strange paradoxes and Jackson said 'Oh Krud",I agree with you on this.

TRINEP 6-8, spacetime

The next day at breakfast we had tofu (soy) eggs and artificially produced steak with newly made real potato pancakes with wheat slices of toast with strawberry jam and coffee and tea. Then after their morning meal they finished the conversion of the survival tent to a hot sauna bath unit and finished the sealing up of the recently opened cave entrance hole. And then checking the intake hose on just under the pond water surface and Ramon said to Peter Walker who was testing the purity of the pond with his chemical composition analyzer tablet computer, and he said it is still pure with no antigens, microbes or anything that can or will harm us.

h) **Franz Waldheim**, m Chief Triton Supervisor and Geologist

j) **Paul Stewart,** m Co-Pilot and Robotics specialist

k) **Arlene Cummings,** f Wellness and Greenhouse Horticulturist

l) **Jennifer Aldridge**, f Nuclear Physicist and System Engineer

m) **Ramon Sanchez**, m Chief Plumber and thermal Electrician

n) **Peter Walker,** m Chief Chemist Hydrologist and Biologist

o) **Mary Walton**, f Medical Doctor and Biologist, and Nutritionist

p) **Anna Magdalena,** f Chief Pilot and Communications Officer

I) **Daxor AI-5 Cyborg Robot,** Chief human formed Android

J) **Laura Philmore** f, Genetic Medical Biologist and Doctor

K) **Jackson Banes** m, Astrophysicist and astronomer

M) **Joanne Collins,** f Mineralogist and chemical Geologist

N) **Jeffrey Watkins**, m Mechanical engineer thorium physicist

O) **Allison Biels**, Robotics, computer engineer, and programming

a) **SHOP (1), Sleeping, LIbrary and resting quarters**

b) **SHOP (2), Mess hall and hospital infirmary**

c) **SHOP (3), Geological facility**

d) **SHOP (4), Chemical facility**

e) **SHOP (5), Robotic, communication and network computer**

f) **SHOP (6), External drilling laboratory facility**

g) **SHOP (7), Garden and greenhouse unit**

h) **SHOP (8), Garage, Nuclear Power and exploratory vehicles center**

i) **SHOP (9), Astronomy and deep space exploration command**

TRINEP 1-9, spacetime

Anna Magdalena is the main Pilot

Paul Stewart is the Co-Pilot and Radar and photography

Daxor is Navigation

Rohn is Communication and flight systems

The next morning after breakfast Franz Waldheim said at their usual morning briefing to the team members and daily work itinerary schedules that we have to take care of the survival tent and somebody here said to me why don't you turn it into a sauna, and I was thinking about that and I may just do that and my other plan is to repair and close the cave entrance hole that I and we made and for us never to go back there ever again. Then Anna Magdalena said what about 'venture', sitting just two hundred miles from here, and he said the spacecraft would simply just sit there for now, and better there than in space orbit where it will be in an orbital conflict with 'Meridien', spacecraft. And then if nobody has any other questions or statements for us let us go now, and we have to do a lot of work today he said. When the work was finished by late afternoon, Jackson Banes said I just received a scramble morse coded message from Earth that we should simply monitor and insure their 'Frontier', space satellite drone reaches Pluto safely and Franz said to Banes in the small kitchen having coffee and tea, thank you for keeping me informed and then Franz said to him the unused tracking antenna and communications disk is doing the tracking of 'Frontier', right and Banes said back to Franz yes it is and should pass us by in the next two days and we will continue to track its planetary route until we can remote from here on Triton put the 'Frontier', space drone satellite in its final orbit on Pluto.

Later that day Franz Waldheim called in Anna Magdalena And Paul Stewart into his small office in SHOP no.1 unit and discussed with them whether we should leave the 'Venture', down in that ravine collecting nitrogen icing coating and possible rusting and with its perfectly good thorium reactors for now going to I believe going to waste, and Both Anna and then Paul said back to him you are quite correct and it is not wise to keep it there unsupervised for to long with a chance of cosmic and Triton cold and wind erosion to cause problems, as you know Franz with Anna speaking back to him that the 'Venture', is our main backup vehicle for us to get back to Earth if our replacements do not arrive here on Triton with its schedule time. And, then Franz said to them I truly believe for now we should put the spacecraft back into our orbit above for now, and they both agreed with Franz who is giving them authorization to retrieve the laying spacecraft and putting it into a safe orbit near Cosmoport base above, and they agreed to do that and said to franz please have Ramon clear and too prepare our capsule shuttle for take off, and Franz said I will intercom him right now, and they said can we take Rohn and Daxor with us, and he said back to them smiling if you want them you got them, and I wish you four good luck.

Over two hours later having blasted off the launch pad,they are now slowly descending down to the ravine valley where they placed their 'Venture', spacecraft and are now hovering going to the rear and under belly of the spacecraft where they opened up the capsule shuttle bay door and gently flew into it and docked in its placement platform flooring and then locking its gripping fasteners they then by remote control put on the lights and heating ducts and stepped out and went to the bridge and once there they then turned on completely the spacecraft engines and flight systems controller with a proper checklist diagnostics calibration before they take off, the last thing they did was to initiate a double redundancy diagnostics of the spacecraft network mult-functions computer and remote control subsystems commands in making sure they have proper AI integrated network computer assistance for take off.

With everything looking good and okay for a take off launch go, Anna Magdalena and Paul Stewart are set to engage for a launch to go, they them revved up their throttle for fuel injection mixing and then Anna increasing the throttle engines and opening yolk and slowly the spacecraft started to move and looking outside they saw the frozen nitrogen come off the spacecraft

With Anna, Paul, Rohn and with Daxor who is now looking not on the falling nitrogen from the spacecraft but with his zoom telephoto eye lens saw in the distance three very large saucer spaceships going and leaving Neptune and towards Uranus, with Daxor recording this in silence, who will later tell Franz Waldheim with his bluetooth connection to the wall display screen in his office for any answers.

And, then they felt the spacecraft now moving completely off the Triton surface ground with Anna then increasing the fuel injection to the four under belly vertical ascend thrusters and now slowly they have increased their take off and are now ascending in moving fast and accelerating now over one thousand feet in the Triton atmosphere and now Anna said to everyone sitting down stay in place we are now a go for complete launch and with the four lift engines are completely revved up to full speed and off they went to over twenty five thousand feet above to park above the Cosmoport, base in a controlled orbit of Triton.

After they set their spacecraft high above orbit of Triton at their stationed Cosmoport, base they then took their capsule space shuttle and departed their spacecraft and gently descended down to their launch pad and returned back to their new home here on Triton and then they parked inside the garage and once inside they handed the capsule shuttle commands with their full control of their password codes to Ramon Sanchez who then parked the capsule shuttle in its parking space, and then later sitting by his command console remote control unit made sure that the 'Venture', is quite comfortable in its new and constant orbit of Triton above the Cosmoport, outpost base.

Later at the Cosmoport, base Daxor came into Franz Waldheim office and asked to speak to him while he was sitting at his desk and Franz said come on in Daxor and he did turning on the screen display and through his Bluetooth transfer interface transferred these pictures of the three alien saucer spacecrafts to his wall screen where Franz Waldheim was then completely a gasped and now mystified at what he is looking at on the screen and then through the base intercom asked Jackson Banes to come into his office. Then a few minutes later Jackson Banes came in and saw on the view screen the three huge saucer spacecraft traveling past Neptune and looking at Daxor and Franz Waldheim, and he said to them who took these pictures and Franz said to him that they were taken by Daxor with his high resolution zoom camera eye lens, and then Jackson said to them I am monitoring the traveling 'Frontier', spacecraft drone that is now headed for Pluto, which has just passed by Neptune, and is now very close to us on Triton and our Cosmoport, Base. And, Jackson said to them do you think they saw our spacecraft drone coming to Neptune, and both Franz and Daxor said to hm, no because if they did see our spacecraft said Franz and in agreement with Daxor who concurred that they would have surely destroyed the spacecraft drone before it would have bypassed the Neptunian planet.

Then Jackson said to them what are they waiting for and if they want to conquer the inner planets of Earth and Mars why haven't they did it already, and Franz Waldheim said perhaps they are somehow in training and or waiting for the go ahead to do so, or even perhaps they are waiting for their space fleet to arrive, to put simply, because three even if they are huge saucer spaceships cannot conquer the inner planets of Earth and Mars. Jackson then said to them this is absolutely crazy that we cannot warn or send a message telling Earth Space Command of the impending danger to them and now Rohn walks in looking for Daxor and then Jackson said to Rohn you are our alien here look at that view screen and Jackson showed these three huge saucer spaceships and Rohn said back to them these are the 'Orikata', space aliens that we crossed in our centuries passed, and he then said to them that they are a dangerous species of reptilian alien that will think of nothing but the destruction and elimination of your human race in their only obtaining food and resources for their needs before they move on to other worlds and solar systems.

Then Jackson said to him, how can we defeat them and he said there is nothing that can defeat them if they were to strengthen their resolve of attack with a massive show of force through their very large space fleet, because these three huge saucer spaceships are scouting ships for their approaching invasion that will come very soon, and I am warning you that they do have over sixty of the most powerful space forces that will and can destroy your human world, Earth.

The next Earth Triton calendar, morning day at their breakfast conference table everyone was happy except for Jackson, Franz and even Rohn who tried their best to enjoy their food when a few minutes after their meal and they were now sipping their coffee and tea, Franz Waldheim stood up at his conference seat and said to everyone in attendance that we are now facing a massive invasion by the 'Orikata', neo-reptilian species that will very soon come to our solar system with an estimate of sixty very large saucer spaceships that according to Rohn are over five thousand feet in diameter and will then venture towards Earth and Mars and we believe (Jackson, Daxor and Rohn) they will assuredly destroy and kill humanity of our two main worlds forever. Then Anna Magdalena spoke and said to Franz Waldheim, how do we warn Earth Space Command, and Franz Waldheim said to her and the rest of the team attending, we cannot for one simple reason, they will not believe us and they will then automatically send a relief team here and replace us in sending our team back to Earth.

Then Rohn spoke and said to everyone at the conference table that I am announcing to you that my duties on board my spaceship was historical junior officer holder for record keeping of our culture, every ship has one as we explore space and I am the holder of our historical battles with the 'Orikata', neo-reptilian aliens and in my life buoy escape capsule I have in my special case that is secured, where I will now hand it over to Daxor who will look into its database contents and perhaps you will find answers in their weakness, but there is one thing that I do know is that the 'Orikata', have one particular weakness and that is they hate the cold, for they are like all cold blooded alien creatures who need warmth, without it they are at sleep and go into a hibernation phase, as they are like all reptilians they only conquer warm solar directed worlds and not planets or moons like Triton where they have no use to ever conquer a cold surfaced like moon and that is why they will never come here and why we are somewhat protected by them in coming here, and then Franz Waldheim said to him why didn't you say this to us before, and Rohm said to him that they were in no way going to invade this solar system before until now, so I kept silent about it until now where I have decided to speak to you about their possible invasion of your star system in there capability to destroy your human race on your world, Earth and Mars.

Later that day in SHOP N0.9 astronomy unit, Jackson was looking at his own database in the last twenty-four hours Earth time, and checking with Nereid asteroid-moon solar system directed telescope, and Cosmoport deep space star gazing telescope and found absolutely nothing and then making sure of his not finding any invasion or saucer spacecraft in our solar system at all or in the vicinity of Pluto and Charon, and one billion miles further into the Kuiper belt, and there was nothing not even a hint of anything involving a future invasion of this solar system by any advanced neo-reptilian species. Then Jackson contacted Franz Waldheim, Daxor and Rohn with Anna Magdalena joining in the conversation on the Cosmoport intercom and ten minutes later they walked into the No.9 astronomy pod unit, and then Jackson said to them that there is no invasion of any kind coming now or next week Earth time, and then Franz Waldheim speaking to Daxor said what does this mean, and Daxor said to them, that I am an AI cyborg robot who cannot fabricated or invent and invasion by these three huge saucers, and what I showed you on the view screen was correct and true in my display bluetooth transfer to you, and then Rohn interrupted and said what I know as an historian of 'Orikata', technology is that they are fully capable of interdimensional phased cloaking and with Franz Waldheim and Jackson speaking, if they have this technology we are really truly in trouble and why these neo-reptilian aliens with there sixty huge saucer spaceships can easily defeat Earth and Mars. And then Rohn said to Jackson and Franz, have you checked there interdimensional phased cloaking frequency signature whose signal that is extremely narrow in its band width, and no matter Rohn said how quiet you make the thrust engines, there is always a slight engine output murmur that gives its location away, but tracking it with an oscilloscope of its signature will be quite noticeable and could be used with any dish antenna aimed directly at them. And, Rohn said you can easily modify your deep space dish antennas to pick up its spatial frequency location simply by tracking its distinct specialized radio-like emitted high or low wave frequency signals to home in on.

Then Jackson said to Rohn and Anna with Daxor can you help me with this distinct radio emitted wave signal, and they all said yes. And, then Franz said to them very well, it looks like you are ahead in finding whether they exist or not and can you give me the results later today or tomorrow Earth time and Jackson Banes said I will be the lead investigator here and Franz Waldheim said okay and then said to them thank you.

After three hours the small group of people (Jackson, Anna, Daxor, Rohn and Paul Stewart and Allison Beils) all helping together in figuring out and getting their Telescopes and deep space dish antennas to find out how to track their specialized engine propulsion signal signatures and at the same time also to monitoring the 'Frontier', spacecraft drone now passing Triton and are now headed to Pluto. With Jackson Banes leading the group and Paul Stewart and Allison Beils have just discovered something very bizarre for they just now uncovered something that will explain that the network computer of Cosmoport has been compromised with a special virus downloaded software type program and what is more astounding is that all of this virus download originated by Daxor who said to everyone what do you mean and Allison Beils said somehow you came in contact with this virus, and then Anna Magdalena said I think I know where he got this virus, and it was with the alien spacecraft trapped in the nitrogen ice that exploded and then Paul said yes that has to be it. And, the Rohn spoke and said proper military procedure is an intruder that enters our spacecraft is to be automatically injected with a virus to preserve and protect our technology and to prevent any alien stealing our spaceships secrets. Then Paul Stewart turned off Daxor completely without his knowledge and later he and Allison Beils will correct his program and return him back to normal with their latest antivirus and malware protection installed package, with allison Beils saying to them all here to do a thorough systems wide virus diagnostics, and they all agreed to do so.

Coming back two hours later Alison Beils and Paul Stewart told Franz Waldheim that they have uncovered and incredible simulation program within.

With these AI infected programs discovered by Daxor, but also our own network computer system too that Daxor infected unknowingly and what we thought was an alien invasion was not at all in our solar system is completely fabricated but now is harmless and safe, but then Franz Waldheim said what about the hologram alien world and they said that while we were sleeping somehow he put on us these entertainment programs and communicator nodule interfaces on the back of our ears. And don't forget Daxor was being manipulated by this alien program from Rohn alien from the very begining comrades and that is why we thought we saw an alien civilization but we didn't we only imagine it after we came back from seeing an empty space in the dark cave then what about the metal alloy that if you look around we don't have it anymore because that too also was fabricated by the program. The only alien we have here is Rohn and that is real and why we are glad that he helped us to unlock and decipher this computer virus program infecting every aspect of our network computer system here at the cosmoport base, and also with the robot Daxor is doing just fine.

The End of Cosmoport

IN MEMORIAM

In honor of my parents, my mother, Anna Magdalena Buhler, and my Father Franz Walter Buhler, who inspired me to do right and to forgive me when I did wrong. That in later years made me an author and I wish to thank them very whole heartily for doing so for me. To a warm and loving parents I thank them, very heartfelt regretfully for their passing away of two wonderful souls and parents, and I miss them to this very day in giving me hope to be a book writer.

www.ingramcontent.com/pod-product-compliance
Lightning Source LLC
Chambersburg PA
CBHW050455110726
47899CB00003B/945